Arkansas
State Facts

Nickname:	The Natural State
Date Entered Union:	June 15, 1836 (the 25th state)
Motto:	*Regnat populus* (The people rule)
Arkansas Men:	William Jefferson Clinton, *U.S. president* Douglas MacArthur, *five-star general* Johnny Cash, *singer*
State Name's Origin:	French interpretation of a Sioux word *acansa,* meaning "downstream place."

Dear Diary,

Tonight I'm going to a party! It's my first real party! There's going to be all kinds of food, a real live band and dancing. Mama saved her money for three months to buy me a new dress and when Morgan sees me in it, he's going to know I'm not just the hillbilly girl who worked at his daddy's sawmill. He's going to see I'm a grown up woman. He's going to notice me...finally.

American

HEROES

AGAINST ALL ODDS

STELLA
BAGWELL

Hillbilly Heart

Silhouette Books

Published by Silhouette Books

America's Publisher of Contemporary Romance

To my brother Lloyd, catering and banquet chef at
Oklahoma University, of whom I'm very proud.
My sister Thelma, who knows me so well and is always
there through thick and thin. My brother Charles,
who is simply a golden guy through and through.
And in loving memory of our sister Harriet.

We miss you, Harri.

SILHOUETTE BOOKS
300 East 42nd St.,
New York, N.Y. 10017

ISBN 0-373-82202-2

HILLBILLY HEART

Copyright © 1989 by Stella Bagwell

This edition published by arrangement with Harlequin Books S.A.

Visit Silhouette at www.eHarlequin.com

Printed in U.S.A.

About the Author

Stella Bagwell sold her first book to Silhouette in November 1985. Now, nearly forty novels later, she is still thrilled to see her books in print and can't imagine having any other job than that of writing about two people falling in love.

She lives in a small town in southeastern Oklahoma with her husband of over twenty-six years. She has one son.

Books by Stella Bagwell

Dear Reader,

Through the years, my books have been inspired by something I've heard, felt or seen. The notion for *Hillbilly Heart* came from the Ouachita (Wash-a-taw) Forest in Arkansas. There in the beautiful mountains, folks live as they have for generations—a simple country life, where rockers sit on front porches, vegetable gardens grow out back, roosters announce the break of day and whippoorwills call on summer nights.

Like many people, the hero of *Hillbilly Heart* believes a person must see more than a home in the Arkansas woods before he or she can truly be happy. But eventually he learns that the quiet view of a piney mountain is enough to satisfy the soul, as long as you're with the person you love. I hope you enjoy reading how Morgan and Lauren finally find a home filled with love in the Ouachita.

Wishing you joy and love,

[signature]

Please address questions and book requests to:
Silhouette Reader Service
U.S.: 3010 Walden Ave., P.O. Box 1325, Buffalo, NY 14269
Canadian: P.O. Box 609, Fort Erie, Ont. L2A 5X3

Prologue

Lauren Magee shut the door of her little economy car with a tired shove of her hip, then reached down to lock it. Shuffling her handbag and raincoat over one arm, she started toward the house. As she walked across the concrete drive and up the steps, a warm Gulf wind rippled through the loose black curls on her shoulders.

It was well into the first week of November, but here in Houston it was just like most other summer nights. The day had been a hot, humid one. Now that the sun had set, the sky was like a muggy black cloak hanging over the city. A hurricane had moved into the Gulf only yesterday. Already the wet wind announced several days of rain ahead.

Lauren stepped through the front door as the memory of crisp autumn days and the crunch of bright-colored leaves beneath her feet traveled through her thoughts. She was homesick. But then, Lauren was always homesick.

In the living room her aunt, a rather plain woman with light brown hair, sat reading quietly in an armchair. She looked up over the rim of her glasses and smiled warmly at Lauren. "You've had a long day. I was beginning to think you might have had trouble on the way home."

Lauren sank gratefully onto the couch, then quickly pulled her thick-soled work shoes off her aching feet and set them aside. Absently she began to massage her cramped toes. Shaking her head, she said, "I had a late perm to do, and a haircut walked in at the last minute. Is Scott already asleep?"

Hattie nodded. "He played hard today with the neighbor's boy. He practically fell asleep in the bathtub."

Lauren sighed. "His mother may have the same problem."

"You work too hard, Lauren. When are you ever going to take a break?"

Now's the time to tell her, Lauren thought. She took a deep breath and said, "I've finally taken your advice, Aunt Hattie, and told Juanita that I need two weeks' vacation."

Her aunt's face brightened perceptibly. "Well, it's about time! Money isn't everything, you know."

Lauren's mouth twisted wryly, but she didn't respond to Hattie's comment. Instead, she said with quiet determination, "I'm going home, Aunt Hattie."

"What are you talking about? You are home."

Lauren shook her head of curly black hair. "Not really." She looked up with a rueful smile. "I'm sounding ungrateful now, aren't I?"

Hattie watched as Lauren continued to massage the ache from her feet. She was a beautiful young woman. Ivory-white skin, raven-black hair and brilliant green eyes were a stunning combination, especially when coupled with a soft, full mouth, high, rounded cheekbones and a slightly dimpled chin. For the past four years Hattie had treated Lauren like the daughter she'd never had. "No, you're not sounding ungrateful," she said. "Just different." The older woman leaned back in the armchair with a thoughtful expression. "Are you trying to tell me you're going back to Mena?"

Lauren straightened on the cushion. "Yes, that is what I'm saying."

Hattie set the newspaper she'd been reading aside. "This is rather sudden, isn't it?"

Wearily Lauren rose to her feet. She was petite, with a figure shapely enough to turn many a male head. But attracting men was the least of her cares or concerns. "Not really. I've been thinking about returning for some time now."

"But why?" Hattie asked, obviously surprised. "It's been well over three years. You've made your home here in Houston. Why go back? Besides visiting your mother, there's nothing there for you."

Lauren frowned. Her aunt's words were certainly true. There wasn't anything there for Lauren except her mother, and her mother had a job at the local school, a circle of friends, her own life to lead.

Yet there might be something in Mena for Scott. She had to keep thinking that, reminding herself that his needs came before her feelings.

"I know I vowed never to go back. But that was a long time ago. And I was very young then." Lauren shrugged and began to walk toward the hallway that led to the kitchen. Hattie quickly got to her feet and followed.

"It's just that you've always been so adamant about your decision to remain here in Houston," Hattie said.

"I'm twenty-two now, Aunt Hattie. I'm beginning to look at things differently."

"Naturally, you're going to look at things differently than you did when you were eighteen. You've matured, grown up, since you left Mena," she told Lauren.

"I certainly hope so," Lauren muttered. As she entered the open doorway on the right, her bare feet suddenly came in contact with cool linoleum. "Is there anything left over from supper? I hope Scott's appetite was good. That stomach virus has left him looking so peaked."

Hattie crossed the large kitchen, which was decorated in bright blue and yellow. Jammed on a counter between the range and the refrigerator was a small microwave oven. She flipped it on and turned back to Lauren. "Scott ate everything on his plate, and so will you. Sit down and rest while I get your coffee and silverware.''

Lauren sat in a chair at the maple table situated at one end of the room. Yellow café curtains were pulled across the windows, blocking Lauren's view of the residential street, which was shrouded now by the darkness of night.

She *had* put in a long day at the salon. Her first appointment had been at 7:30, more than thirteen hours ago, and she was feeling the effects of standing on her feet for all those long hours.

Slowly she pushed her hands against the small of her back and arched her shoulders in an effort to relax the tight muscles.

By the time Hattie had placed a steaming mug of coffee in front of Lauren, the bell on the microwave had pinged. "Barbecued ribs. I can already smell them,'' Lauren said.

Hattie smiled smugly and carried the plate of food over to her niece. "Wrong, my dear. Barbecued brisket, coleslaw and hot rolls, so eat up.''

The scent of the food wafted up to Lauren's nose. Her mouth watered hungrily as she picked up her fork. At lunch she'd only had the chance to swallow a few bites of chicken sandwich. Her empty stomach had been gnawing at her painfully for the past few hours.

After swallowing a bite of the deliciously tender brisket, Lauren looked over at her aunt, who was busy unloading clean dishes from the dishwasher. "Actually, I must be out of mind to consider going home for two weeks. If I stayed here you'd wait on me and pamper me like a baby." Lauren spoke in a half-teasing manner, but she couldn't have been more sincere.

"Lauren, I— You really are serious about this, aren't you?"

Hattie pulled out a chair across from Lauren and sank into the cushioned seat. Her brown eyes were filled with surprise and concern when she turned them on her niece. It had been a long, hard road for Lauren. She didn't want to see her hurt any more than she'd been already.

Lauren nodded at her aunt and said softly, "I've been thinking so much about Scott lately. And each time I think about— Well, what is he going to think when he gets older, Aunt Hattie? How will I explain things?"

Hattie shook her head. "My word, Lauren, the child won't even be three until January. He's too young to understand much of anything right now."

Frowning, Lauren lifted a roll from her plate and spread it with thick, sweet butter. "That's what you think. He sees other children with their fathers. He wants to know where his is, why he doesn't have one, too."

"Are you telling me that you intend to go back to Mena because of Morgan?" Hattie's voice was full of shock. This was the last thing she expected from Lauren.

Frowning, Lauren stabbed at the brisket. "What do you mean, because of Morgan?"

"I mean, are you still harboring feelings for Morgan Sinclair?"

Feelings! That was certainly too mild a word for what she felt toward Morgan Sinclair. "No! Scott deserves to know who his father is. And maybe...well, maybe," she added in a softer tone, "Morgan should know he has a son. Even if he doesn't care about him."

"I can't imagine anyone not caring for a child," Hattie said. She leaned back in her chair. "Still, you've never before wanted him to know about the baby. Why now?"

Lauren winced as a pang of conscience twisted inside her. It was true that she'd never wanted Morgan to know about Scott. She'd left Mena with a broken heart, trying desperately to hate Morgan because he hadn't wanted her enough to marry her. The last thing Lauren had wanted to do was to tell him about the baby and force him to marry her out of a sense of obligation. It would have made a mockery of everything she held precious.

Time might not mend broken hearts, she thought, but it did alter things. "Scott isn't going to be a baby forever. I don't want him growing up believing I deliberately kept him from his father or blaming me for his being—" She couldn't finish the sentence.

She didn't have to. Hattie did it for her. "Illegitimate?"

"It still has an ugly sound to it, doesn't it?" Lauren said. "Even now, when moral and social standards are so much more relaxed."

Hattie grimaced. "Lauren, dear, you're a wonderful mother to Scott. There's no way he could ever blame you for anything."

Lauren's shoulders lifted, then sagged. She looked at her plate and said, "I want Scott to have all the good things he deserves. I don't want him to have to pay for my mistake."

"Mistake? All you did was fall in love. That isn't a sin, you know."

Lauren's soft lips twisted in self-mockery. "No. Falling in love isn't a sin. But trusting Morgan with my love was a mistake. A costly, foolish mistake on my part."

Lauren rarely talked about Scott's father. Even now, after all this time, Hattie was reluctant to mention his name around Lauren. She remembered all too well the tears it used to produce in her niece's eyes. Hattie had never met the man, nor did she particularly want to. He'd broken Lauren's heart and left her with a child, and he hadn't once tried to contact her since she'd left Mena. In Hattie's opinion, Scott could do without a father like that.

"Then I can't imagine you wanting to go back. There are thousands of men here in Houston. You could have your pick, Lauren. I know there's a good man out there who would love Scott like his own."

Lauren lifted her fork to her mouth automatically. "There probably is, but I don't want him."

Hattie's fine brows lifted. "Then what do you want, Lauren? Do you still want Morgan? Is that why you've suddenly decided to go home?"

Lauren's head jerked up. "No! That's the last thing I want," she cried.

Hattie threw her hands in the air. "You're going to let this one experience with a man warp you for life? That's rather stupid thinking, isn't it?"

Lauren put down her fork and wearily rubbed her forehead. She hadn't meant to get into this kind of discussion tonight. But she should have expected it. She should have known Hattie wouldn't take her decision to go back home lightly.

"Look, Aunt Hattie, I've got two weeks' vacation coming. It would be nice to spend it with Mother. It would be nice for Mother to spend it with Scott. And maybe—if things seem right—I'll tell Morgan about his son."

Hattie looked unconvinced. "Then you're not planning on returning to Arkansas permanently?"

"No," Lauren answered with a shake of her head. "Good heavens, my job is here. My life is here now."

"It would be easy for you to get a job as a hairdresser in Mena. That friend of yours, Gypsy, has been after you for a long time to work in her salon. And Lord knows how much Eileen would love to have you back home to stay."

Lauren's expression was suddenly firm. "Maybe Mother would like it. But it's out of the question." There was no way she wanted to be that close to Morgan. Letting him know about Scott was one thing; putting herself in a position where she might run into him at any time was quite another.

With a worried little frown, Hattie rose from the

table. "Well, that should make me feel relieved. But I can tell you, Lauren, I don't like this idea at all. I think it's something you need to think over very carefully. After all, I don't think any man would be very happy about being kept in the dark about his own offspring."

Lauren let out a deep breath and reached for her fork. "When I came down here I didn't realize I was pregnant. You know that. And Morgan had already made it clear he wanted me out of his life." She shrugged and fought to keep the pain from her voice. "He may not even want to know now. It's hard to tell about that. I thought I knew him once. But.... At any rate, I'm not telling him about Scott to make him happy."

"Then why are you telling him? To ease your conscience?"

"Aunt Hattie!"

"Well, it's the only reason I can think of."

"Scott is the reason," Lauren said.

Hattie slowly shook her head. "Have you considered that Morgan might press for parental rights? What would you do then?"

Lauren's face paled to a paper white, but she laughed brittlely. "Morgan would never do that. It would be too embarrassing for him."

Hattie lifted a hand in a helpless gesture. "What do you want from him, then? What do you stand to gain by telling him about Scott?"

For a moment Lauren stared across the room, her thoughts, her heart, remembering. What did she want from Morgan? She had wanted so much back then. And he'd been unable to give her anything—except Scott. For that much she was grateful. Her son was the only thing she lived for. She glanced up and saw her aunt's pinched expression. "I want Scott to know he has a real father. If he sees Morgan, it will make it real for him. His father won't be just some vague figure in his imagination. And as far as wanting something from Morgan is concerned, I don't. I'd like for him to be willing to acknowledge Scott on his birthdays or the holidays, but nothing more than that."

Hattie snorted. "Why not just pick a man off the street? He could do that much for you."

By now Lauren had lost her appetite. She put her fork aside and rose tiredly. "I lied to Morgan by keeping Scott's birth a secret, but I will never lie to my son. His life is going to begin with the truth. I'm going to see to that much."

Chapter One

Mena, Arkansas was nestled in the mountains at the edge of the Ouachita National Forest—a long way from Houston in more than just distance. A town with a population of five thousand couldn't compare with a city of more than a million people. Lauren had grown up on the outskirts of Mena. Now, as she drove through the mountains on Highway 71, she realized how much she had missed the forest.

Most of the foliage had already changed color with the fall weather. The leaves were beginning to fall. But in many places sweet gums stood in scarlet majesty, and maples and hickories competed for attention with their golden splendor.

Living in Houston had almost made Lauren forget how beautiful Mena was. Almost, but not quite. She hadn't forgotten anything about home, about her family and friends and, most of all, she hadn't forgotten anything about Morgan. But she didn't want to think about Morgan at the moment. It was enough to drive slowly through the steep, winding crooks and turns in the highway and enjoy the late-evening sunshine.

On the seat beside her, Scott lay sleeping. He'd stayed awake for most of the trip, but after they'd stopped to eat in Longview, Texas, his eyelids had grown heavier and heavier, and he'd finally succumbed to a full tummy and the monotonous hum of the car's engine.

Lauren's lips curved with fierce maternal pride as she glanced down at him. Everyone said Scott looked like her. She supposed that was because his hair was nearly as black as hers and just as curly. And already his eyes were darkening to a deep green. Still, Lauren could see subtle hints of Morgan in her son's features. His skin tanned to a deep brown like Morgan's, whereas hers always remained a milky white. The angle of his jaw had that certain stubborn thrust to it, and then there were the faint bump at the bridge of his nose and the deep dimple to the left of his mouth.

Yet Lauren doubted anyone would pick up on these things unless he was looking for them. As yet, she hadn't decided what she would say if anyone back in Mena questioned her about Scott's father. She was hoping her old friends would have more tact. At any rate, it would all depend on Morgan.

It had been nearly four years since she'd left Mena, and Lauren had no idea how he'd react to her, much less Scott. Given the way they had parted, she suspected he would consider her return a nuisance. That

would be fine with Lauren. She hoped she could look
at him and feel nothing at all. She hoped she could
tell him about Scott in a cool, emotionless manner
that would prove to him that she no longer loved him.

No longer loved him. The words mocked her
heart—mocked everything inside her. She didn't want
Scott to begin his life with any kind of deceit, yet she
was still lying to herself. Still trying to tell herself she
didn't love Morgan. But her heart recognized the lie.
It throbbed with aching hunger at the merest thought
of him.

Eileen Magee, Lauren's mother, lived south of
town on a gravel country road. As Lauren flipped on
the turn signal and veered off the main highway, her
heartbeat picked up its pace. She was anxious to see
her mother and her old home. It seemed so long ago
that she'd packed and left the only home she had ever
known. She'd missed it fiercely, but she'd done her
best to keep that from Hattie and Bob.

They had done everything humanly possible to
make their home Lauren's home, too, and she loved
them for it. But Arkansas was in her blood, just as
Morgan was, she supposed. Perhaps she felt that way
because home and growing up and Morgan were all
interwined and could never be separated.

The road was full of gaping potholes. Lauren
slowed the car and did her best to maneuver around
them. Scott must have felt the changed movement of
the car. He squirmed on the seat, then finally opened
his eyes.

"Hello, sleepyhead," Lauren said with a tender

smile. "Are you going to wake up in time to see Grandma?"

The young man rubbed his eyes with his fists, then scrambled up to a sitting position. "Grandma," he repeated, looking eagerly out the window. "Are we there, Mama?"

Lauren nodded. "Almost, honey. Just around this next curve and down the hill. Then you'll see Grandma's house."

He scooted to the edge of the seat and blinked sleepily. "We're up high," he said in an awed little voice.

Lauren stifled a chuckle. These hills probably did seem high to Scott. All he'd ever seen was the flatlands of Texas.

"Yes, we're up a little higher now. How do you like all the trees?"

"There's lots!" He turned an excited face to his mother. "Is there a squirrel in there, Mama? Can we see one?"

She smiled indulgently and patted his cheek. "There are lots of squirrels. You might see one if you keep watching."

He pressed his nose eagerly to the window. Lauren knew then that she'd made the right decision in bringing Scott back home. Young or old, a person needed roots. And she wanted these mountains to be Scott's roots. His family was here, and that would be important to him.

It made Lauren happy to see him so enthralled by their surroundings. When she pulled up next to the front gate of the old farmhouse, she was just as excited as Scott was.

"Grandma! Grandma!"

Before the child could rush through the gate, Eileen Magee was already through the front door and down the steps. She was a tall woman with fiery red hair and a fair complexion. A smile lit her pretty features, which were still smooth and youthful looking.

"Come here, my little darlin'," she cried happily.

Lauren pushed open the gate leading to the walk. Scott scrambled through it and flung himself into his grandmother's arms.

The redheaded woman laughed and lifted him up in the air. "My goodness, Scott, I'm going to have to put a rock on your head! You're just getting too big!"

The boy giggled and glanced proudly back at his mother. "I'm gonna be three soon," he told his grandmother.

"Three! Are you sure you're telling me right? You can't be that old!"

Scott nodded with great seriousness. "Yep. I'm gonna be three. Mama's gonna let me go to school!"

"School?" Eileen glanced confusedly over at her daughter, and Lauren smiled.

"Nursery school," she explained.

"Oh, I see," Eileen said, setting Scott back on his feet but still holding on to his hand. She leaned over to receive Lauren's kiss on the cheek. "It's so wonderful to have you back home, honey. You can't imagine what it means to me."

"It feels wonderful to be here, Mom. Everything looks beautiful—especially you."

Eileen blushed and turned to lead Scott into the house. "Let's go in," she said happily, "and you can tell me all about the drive up."

"If you don't mind," Lauren said, "I'd love to look around for a minute."

Eileen nodded with gentle understanding, then turned to urge her grandson up the wooden steps and across the wide porch. When they'd gone inside, Lauren lifted her head and sniffed appreciatively at the clean, pine-scented air.

That fresh, crisp smell of country woods had never left her memory in all the time she'd been away in Houston. She filled her lungs with it now, while her eyes took in the vibrant foliage. A crepe myrtle stood at one end of the porch. It's leaves were still intact, but they'd turned a deep violet-red.

Lauren stepped off the walk and began a slow, meandering tour of the rest of the yard. It was small, boxed off from the woods with a barbed-wire fence. Behind the house was a huge loblolly pine. It shaded most of the screened-in porch, as well as the well-house. Her mother had scolded Lauren many times for climbing it and smearing her clothes and hair with pine resin.

The memory brought a faint smile to Lauren's lips, but the smile quickly faded when she rounded the house and looked down the road. Two miles farther on was the Sinclair Mill. She wondered if it still looked the way it had when she and Morgan used to carry away the pine slabs there. That was very doubt-ful, she thought. Everything was probably mecha-nized now, with machines to do much of the manual labor.

Morgan had always been ambitious. And since he'd inherited the mill after his father's death a couple of years ago, he'd probably expanded the whole place. Lauren's mother had told her that he'd bought several tracts of land between here and the mill. He was ob-viously doing well for himself. But then, that came as no surprise to Lauren. The Sinclairs had always been rich. What with the lumber mill and their truck-ing firm, they'd never lacked money.

Memories, sweet and tender, stabbed her with fresh pain. Morgan had been her whole life for such a long time that these past four years had not really seemed like living. She'd merely been existing, pushing her-self to function for the sake of her son.

Maybe, in time, she would be able to forget. Maybe coming home after so long would help exorcise Mor-gan from her heart. But she doubted that such a mir-acle would happen. For the moment, she would settle for getting through the next two weeks without break-ing apart.

"I'm so glad you're having cool weather up here," Lauren said later that night. "It's been a long time since I've been able to sit in front of the fire and soak up the warmth."

After supper, Eileen had built a fire in the fireplace. It was a joy for Lauren to watch the logs crackle and burn. There was never an opportunity in Houston's warm weather to enjoy a fire. Bob and Hattie's house didn't have a fireplace, and even if it had, buying firewood would be very extravagant.

"A long time since you've had woodsmoke in your hair?" Eileen chuckled. "I guess that wouldn't be a good advertisement for a hairdresser." She looked across the room to where Lauren sat cross-legged on the braided rug by the stone hearth. Orange flames danced behind her, highlighting her halo of black curls. "How's business been going?"

"Very good. I've managed to put quite a bit in savings. Of course, Hattie and Bob make it so easy for me to save. The only expenses I have are transportation, clothes and a few medical bills."

Hattie and Eileen were sisters, yet they had very different personalities. Lauren had always thought it comical that her mother was the one with the red hair, because Hattie had the feisty personality and Eileen was quiet and easygoing.

Lauren's father had passed on many years ago, when Lauren had been very small. She couldn't actually remember anything about him. That was another one of the reasons she wanted Scott to know his father.

"They want to make it easy for you, honey," Eileen said. "Their sons are grown and gone. You and Scott have filled their lives."

"They were there when I needed them the most," Lauren said. "I'll always be grateful for that."

Eileen studied her daughter thoughtfully. "You know, Hattie is very worried about you."

Lauren turned a surprised look on her mother. "Worried about me? What do you mean?"

Eileen shrugged. "About this thing with Scott and Morgan."

"She told you about that?"

"She's afraid for you, darling. She's afraid you're going to stir up a hornet's nest and get stung in the process."

Lauren grimaced and turned back to the fire. "What do you think?"

Eileen's face was full of concern. "I never liked the idea of you keeping Scott a secret from Morgan. But now, I...well, it isn't for me to say."

Lauren's throat tightened. "He isn't married, is he?"

"Lands, no! I would have told you."

Lauren hated how relieved she was to hear that Morgan had not yet made some woman his wife.

His wife. She had prayed, dreamed, lived, for the time when she would become Mrs. Morgan Sinclair. God, how foolish that had been!

"Do you ever see him? Talk with him?"

"At times." Eileen lifted the misshapen piece of knitting lying on her lap. "'Course, with me working at the school cafeteria, I don't have much chance to see anyone, except on weekends. But sometimes Morgan stops by on the way to the mill. We have a nice chat now and then."

This news took Lauren completely by surprise. But

perhaps it shouldn't have. Morgan had always thought
very highly of her mother.

"You—you haven't mentioned Morgan to Scott,
have you?" Eileen asked.

Lauren glanced over her shoulder to see her mother
counting stitches. "No. When he asks about his father
I just tell him he lives a long distance away from us
and that sometime we'll go for a visit. He doesn't
know that visit is now."

"Neither does Morgan." Her mother spoke softly.

Even though the heat of the flames was seeping
into her tired body, Lauren shivered. "I just want to
see him, Mom. And when I look in his face I'll know
whether he should be told about Scott."

"I hope you're right, Lauren."

So do I, Lauren silently tacked on. Aloud she said,
"Let's not worry about it now, Mom. I'm going to
be here for two weeks. A lot can happen in that
time."

Eileen grimaced. "That's what worries me."

Sighing, Lauren shifted and lay down on the rug.
Resting her cheek on her arm, she stared into the
flames and said, "I'm sorry I'm worrying you and
Aunt Hattie. But this is just something I feel compelled to do."

Eileen sent her daughter a tender look. "I know
you do, darling. I can even understand why. I only
wish you'd done it in the beginning."

Lauren didn't reply. She watched the fire and re-
called the time she'd discovered she was pregnant
with Morgan's child. The news had stunned her and

filled her with all sorts of emotions. She'd been exhilarated and happy at the thought of a new little being growing inside her, especially because it was part of Morgan. But on the other hand she'd been overwhelmed by the responsibility that lay before her.

Hattie, Bob and her mother had practically begged her to inform Morgan about the baby, and at one point Lauren had almost come back to Mena to let him know. But she kept remembering that he'd told her to go away—anywhere, as long as it was away from him.

She'd made the only choice she could back then, she thought. But now she was older and better able to cope with things, especially since the break with Morgan wasn't so raw and fresh. One way or the other, she would make sure he knew that she hadn't wanted him on terms of pure obligation in the past, and that she wanted nothing from him now.

Lauren and her mother talked for another hour before they decided to go to bed. Scott had been asleep for hours, and after Lauren had showered she moved quietly around the bedroom so as not to wake him.

The room was growing chilly as the falling temperature outside dropped. Her mother had put two more quilts on the bed to give them extra warmth. Lauren didn't remember how heavy the quilts were until she slipped into bed beside her son.

Before she turned out the lamp, Lauren studied Scott's cherubic little face. After several moments passed, she finally reached out with one finger and traced the faint black brows above his closed eyes. This was her son *and* Morgan's. Would Morgan even care?

Chapter Two

Lauren had almost forgotten how cold a frosty November morning could be in Mena. She and Scott lay in her old four-poster, snuggled beneath the three heavy quilts, when Eileen tapped on the door.

It wasn't daylight yet, but Lauren had been awake for some time. She looked up as her mother peered around the door.

"Lauren, I'm leaving for work." She was whispering in order not to wake Scott. "There's coffee already made, and eggs and bacon in the fridge. Fix whatever you want."

"Okay, Mom. See you later."

When Eileen closed the door, Lauren slipped out from under the patchwork quilts and reached for her chenille robe. The hardwood floor was cold under her bare feet as she struggled to push her arms into the twisted sleeves.

The kitchen was warm, and the smell of coffee and toast lingered in the air. Lauren found a mug and poured herself a cup from the drip coffee maker.

Scott would wake in a few minutes. She'd wait to eat breakfast with him. Until then, she was just going to sip her coffee and enjoy the feeling of being home again, of rising early in the morning to a frosty view of the mountains outside the kitchen windows.

For the past four years, Lauren had worked six days a week. Except for the few short weeks she'd taken off to recover from Scott's birth, this was her first real vacation. When she'd discovered she was pregnant, Lauren had quickly decided to attend a trade school and earn a license in cosmetology. It was something she'd had a natural talent for, and it was a way of making a decent living for herself and her child.

Still, in spite of what she'd told her mother about saving money, she didn't really feel she could afford this time away from her job.

However, home and Morgan and Scott had been weighing heavily on her mind. For months she'd harbored the idea of returning to Mena and telling Morgan he had a son. The doubt and indecision had swayed in her mind like a bridge over a treacherous canyon, and the reasons not to tell him had outweighed the positive points of such a choice.

It hadn't been until one of Lauren's steady clients told her of her son's death overseas that she'd actually made up her mind. The man had been serving in the navy, and while he'd been away his wife had given birth to their daughter. He'd never had the chance to see his own child.

Just keeping Scott's birth a secret from Morgan gave Lauren enough guilt to carry. She'd never be able to bear it if something should happen to either Morgan or Scott without the truth being revealed. It was too late to change many things in her life, but in this one area there was still time.

Morgan had regretted making love to Lauren. She'd never forget the hard, unyielding look on his face when he'd told her he wanted nothing more to do with her. The memory of it still had the power to send little shards of pain through her young heart.

Lauren pulled a chair out from the kitchen table and sipped thoughtfully at her coffee.

She supposed she'd been so blinded by love for Morgan that she'd failed to see that it was all one-sided. And that night—the night Scott had been conceived—she'd practically thrown herself at him. She could see that now. But that night had been mystical to Lauren.

It was the first dress-up party she'd ever been to. Her mother had saved for three months to buy Lauren an appropriate dress for the graduation party for Morgan's sister, Dianne. Lauren was graduating in the same high-school class, and Morgan had invited her to attend the party, too.

There had been a band and dancing and all kinds of food Lauren had never seen before, much less tasted. Morgan had been dressed in a dark, elegant suit that enhanced his tanned skin and dark blond hair.

To her, he'd looked like a prince, and she'd known that all the girls at the party were panting after him. He was a Sinclair, and on top of that he was gorgeous. But he'd belonged to Lauren. She'd felt secure in that fact, even though no one else had known it.

She'd been in love with him ever since she'd been seventeen. That night she'd put on the pale lilac dress that revealed her bare shoulders knowing Morgan would take one look at her in it and want her.

And he *had* wanted her, Lauren thought, her fingers tightening painfully around the coffee mug. He'd danced every dance with her. He'd introduced her to all his friends, and he'd told her how beautiful she looked. In short, he'd kept her by his side all night, teasing her, charming her, making her laugh as no one else ever could. Lauren had been glowing with love for him.

It had not shocked or surprised her when, later that night, their kisses had turned into something more passionate. The sexual tension between them had been growing stronger each time they were together. Morgan's kisses had promised so much more, and that night she'd wanted to taste all of his love.

Lauren rose quickly, trying her best to dispel the memories. She'd learned the hard way that giving your body to the man you loved didn't necessarily mean you could expect a commitment from him. Far from it, she thought bitterly.

"Mama, I'm cold."

Lauren looked up to see Scott entering the kitchen, dragging one of the quilts along with him. She smiled at the sight of him in his red long johns, shivering as if there were snow on the ground instead of frost.

"This isn't like being at Uncle Bob and Aunt Hattie's house, is it?" she asked.

"No," he said. His teeth chattered, making Lauren chuckle.

She lifted him into one of the chairs and tucked the quilt around him until nothing was showing but his face and his curly black hair.

"You'll warm up in a minute," she assured him. "Ready for some eggs and toast?"

He nodded. Then his eyes wide, he asked her, "Do you have to go to work, Mama?"

Smiling, Lauren shook her head. No doubt he thought today would be like all the other days she went off to the salon. "No. Mama is on vacation. And when you're on vacation, that means you don't go to work. And it also means that you and I are going to have today and a whole bunch more days to spend together. How does that sound?" she asked, placing her finger on the tip of his nose.

"Yay!" He giggled as Lauren crossed to the refrigerator. She rarely had enough time to spend with her son. Working to take care of his material needs didn't leave much time to merely enjoy being a mother. She was looking forward to these two weeks with Scott, even though the thought of seeing Morgan hung over her like a threatening cloud.

"What do you say you and me go into town this morning and go shopping?" she asked Scott a few minutes later while they ate bacon and eggs.

"Will you buy me a toy?"

"Maybe," she said, struggling to keep a serious look on her face. "Will you be a good boy?"

He nodded and gulped his milk, then wiped away the white mustache it left behind with the back of his hand. "Aunt Hattie says I'm the best little boy in Texas!"

Lauren arched an eyebrow. "Really? Well, Texas is a pretty big state. Do you think she exaggerated a bit?"

"Exa— Exerg— What is that word, Mama?"

Lauren laughed and gave his nose a little pull. "Well, it sorta means stretching the truth. You remember when Joey said you were the one who smeared mud on the car windows, when actually it was him?"

Scott nodded somberly. "He *lied*."

"Well, yes, I guess he did," Lauren said, thinking that although Scott was not even three years old he was already showing personality traits like his father's. Morgan had always been direct and to the point—sometimes painfully so. Especially when he'd told her to go away and grow up.

Well, she'd gone away, she'd had his child, and she hoped she'd grown up in the process. Now the only thing left to do was let Morgan know it.

While Lauren had been away in Houston, several new shopping centers had been built on the northeast side of town. She and Scott explored a few of them until he was tired and whining for lunch, and then they drove to a fast-food place where she ordered burgers and fries for them both.

While they waited for their order, she took off his hooded sweatshirt and shed her own light jacket. Living in Houston, they didn't need many clothes for cooler weather. The white sweater and red corduroy slacks she was wearing today were quite old, but, thankfully, they were still in style.

The morning had turned into a beautiful one. Sunlight streamed through the plate-glass windows beside their booth. Lauren leaned back in the seat and watched Scott push the airplane she'd bought him earlier across the tabletop.

So far, she hadn't run into anyone she knew. She didn't know whether to be sad or relieved. Most of her friends had moved away from Mena, she supposed. But there were still a few around like Gypsy. She thought she might drive by and see her old friend before she and Scott left town. Perhaps Gypsy could come out for supper with them. It had been so long since she'd spent time with someone her own age, so long since she'd taken the time to talk and laugh.

The food came, and she and Scott began to enjoy their lunch.

At the opposite end of the long room, a man sat across from a blond woman. The woman was talking animatedly, even though the man wasn't paying particularly close attention.

"It's going to be a real Thanksgiving bash! What do you say? Do you think you can make it?" she asked.

He looked at the slinky blonde with a faint quirk
on his thin lips. "I haven't had a chance to discuss
Thanksgiving with my family yet. I'll let you know."

That wasn't exactly what she'd wanted to hear, but
the woman settled for it anyway. She smiled and said,
"Good. Because I'm really looking forward to it. And
I know Julie would just love for you to come. You
know, this is her first party since her divorce. Poor
thing, she's just now getting her credit cards back in
order since that monster left her. Do you know
she…"

Bored with her gossip, the man lifted the Styrofoam cup to his lips, sipped hot coffee and let his
eyes wander around the room.

A child's laughter rang out, pulling his attention to
a booth in the opposite corner. A woman was making
a game of feeding ketchup-coated French fries to a
young boy. Once or twice she accidentally smeared
his cheek, making him giggle even louder.

Something about the pair touched him, and he
watched for a moment as the woman reached out and
wiped the child's face clean with a napkin. From
where he was sitting, he couldn't quite see the
woman's face, but the boy's was in plain sight. He
was a cute thing, with curly black hair and a wide
grin that showed off a set of pearly-white baby teeth.
The woman had long, curly black hair, too, that just
brushed the top of her shoulders. A red bandanna had
been twisted into a tight rope and knotted in it. It was
beautiful, glossy hair, just like—

For a moment everything went still inside him.

Across the table, Angela was still droning on, but he was unaware of her words.

No, it couldn't be, he thought. He studied the woman through narrowed eyes, remembering, comparing. The tilt of her head, the set of her shoulders, were the same. But this woman was thinner.

He shook his head. This had happened to him many times before. It wasn't her this time, just as it hadn't been her any of the other times, he told himself. He looked back at Angela just as the woman across the room laughed.

His face paled. He knew that laugh. Hadn't it haunted him for the past four years? He set his coffee aside and rose.

"I'll be back in a minute," he muttered to Angela, leaving her gaping.

Lauren didn't notice that anyone was approaching the table until it was too late. When she heard his voice, her heartbeat, her breath, seemed to freeze in her breast.

"Lauren? That is you, isn't it?"

Slowly she turned her head. "Morgan."

The whisper of his name snapped something inside her. As she looked at him, her heart lurched into a sickening gallop.

He stood there looking at her as though she were a phantom, or some freak of his imagination. It was hard for him to believe that after all this time it was really her.

"How are you, Lauren?"

Her face felt frozen. She forced herself to smile and

hoped it didn't look stiff. "I'm doing very well, Morgan. And you?"

"The same."

The same. Was he still the same Morgan she'd loved so deeply? "Actually, I'm on vacation. So I'm up here visiting Mother," she said, not knowing what else to say.

He reached into his pocket for a cigarette, and Lauren noticed that his body was still as fit as ever. Tall, heavily muscled, without an ounce of fat. She knew he was twenty-eight now. The years had added character to his face, making it more than just smooth and handsome. His unruly, sandy hair was still just as thick and shiny as she remembered.

Morgan slowly struck a match, then cupped his hand around the flame as he brought it to the end of the cigarette. Through squinted copper-brown eyes, he studied her face.

Lauren was even more beautiful now than she'd been when she'd left Mena so long ago. Her face had slimmed, making her cheekbones much more pronounced. It gave her green eyes an exotic slant. Her skin was still flawless and ivory-pale. When he looked at her now, she was everything he'd remembered and more.

"Your mother tells me you make your home in Houston now."

"Yes. I have relatives there." Her fingers lifted and toyed with the curls lying against her collar. "I was sorry to hear about your father. He was a fine man. I'm sure you must miss him terribly."

"I looked for you at the funeral."

That surprised her, but she was struggling not to show it. "I didn't get the news until it was too late."

"Does that mean you might have come?"

Her eyes met his, and the clash jolted her. She was forced to glance away in order to speak. "I—I work six days a week. It's rather hard for me to get away."

"You work?" he asked as if that were the last thing he'd expected her to be doing.

Lauren fought to keep from grimacing at the question. What in hell did he think she would be doing? she wondered. Then she realized she wasn't being fair. Morgan had no idea what kind of life she'd been leading.

"Yes," she said quietly. "I work as a hairdresser now." She looked at him with a wry twist to her lips. "Quite a change from bucking slabs, wouldn't you say?"

His brown eyes softened, and he grinned faintly, making some of the cold stiffness in Lauren's limbs begin to ease.

"Yes, I would say that's quite a change," he murmured.

From the glint in his eyes, Lauren knew he was remembering their times together at the mill, back when she'd been young and a little tomboyish. He'd teased her mercilessly. She was remembering her earlier self, too, and it sent a faint pink color across her cheeks.

"Mama, can I have ice cream?"

Scott's voice broke the moment. Lauren looked

across at her son, knowing that Morgan was staring at the child. Scott openly returned the man's gaze.

And suddenly Lauren felt very sad, as she realized that her son was looking at his father and didn't even know it. To him, this was just a man he'd never seen before.

"Can I, Mama? I want strawberry."

Lauren let out the breath she'd been holding. "After you've finished your lunch."

"But I have. See?"

Lauren glanced at his plate and realized he had eaten everything. "Okay. In a minute," she promised him.

"This is your son?"

Slowly Lauren lifted her head and looked at Morgan again. Her face full of pride, she said, "Yes. This is my son, Scott."

Morgan had believed he'd experienced pain before in his life, but obviously he hadn't. Looking at Lauren and her child, he realized that nothing could compare to the crushing pain rushing through him now. It was illogical, he knew, but he felt cheated, violated in the most intimate way. It was impossible to keep the sarcasm from his voice when he spoke.

"Your mother didn't mention that you were married."

Determined to get through this with as much pride as possible, she held his gaze. "I'm not."

His nostrils flared as his eyes darted from her to Scott, then back to her again. "You didn't let any grass grow under your feet, did you Lauren?'' He spoke softly, accusingly.

Out of all the people Lauren knew, she had never believed Morgan would be the one to condemn her. And how dare he? How dare he? she thought furiously, when he was the man who had taken her innocence, filled her with love, filled her with child, then turned away from her! At that moment she almost hated him.

She turned blindly to Scott and began guiding his arms into his sweatshirt. "It's time for us to go, Scott."

"I want ice cream," he whined.

"Later," she said, reaching for her coat and purse.

Morgan watched her scoop the child up in one arm and get to her feet. He knew he'd offended her, but he didn't care. He'd loved her madly. He'd wanted everything good and right for her. Seeing her unmarried and with a child was a hell of a slap in the face.

"Goodbye, Morgan," she said coolly, stepping around him.

He turned and watched her walk out the double glass doors with the child still in her arms. The faint frown on his face didn't begin to express the turbulence inside him. He returned to Angela.

"What was that all about?" she asked huffily. She wasn't used to having a man leave her sitting alone while he flirted with another woman.

Morgan turned to the blonde, a vacant look in his eyes. "I'd like to know myself," he muttered, throwing her completely off guard.

"Come on," he added. "Let's get out of here."

I must have been out of my mind to think Morgan might want to know he has a child, Lauren thought furiously as she headed her little red car out of town. He was nothing but a judgmental ass!

Scott sat strapped in the seat beside his mother, licking the ice-cream cone she'd bought him before leaving town. He grinned beguilingly up at her, and Lauren smiled back, in spite of the pink stickiness all over his face. Love swelled inside her, and she knew that no matter what course her life might take, her son would always be its center. She was going to make sure he was kept safe and happy, whatever the cost.

By the time she reached her mother's house, she was aware of just how much the meeting with Morgan had taken out of her. She felt weak and drained, and in spite of her anger, she wanted to burst into tears.

She knew it was ridiculous for her to feel this way. Morgan had made it plain to her four years ago that she wasn't the woman for him. Still, she hadn't expected him to be so—so dry, so unlike the Morgan she used to know.

Lauren spent the rest of the afternoon prowling restlessly around the house while Scott played with his toys in front of the fireplace.

She tackled all the housecleaning she could find. Then, for lack of anything else to do, she decided to bake a chocolate cake for their supper.

It was too late to invite Gypsy over, but that was just as well, she decided. The encounter with Morgan had left her in no mood to visit with an old friend. In fact, she could scarcely think. All she could do was turn the words they'd exchanged over and over in her mind.

Now, after she'd had a chance to cool off, she was beginning to have second thoughts about Morgan's behavior. After all, he didn't know Scott was his son. He'd been looking at the child in a totally different light. Scott was small for his age, and questioning the timing of Scott's birth apparently had not occurred to Morgan. Obviously he thought she'd gone to Houston and stepped into the fast lane. It was incredible for him to believe that of her. They had been so close for so long! For two years they had been friends, constant companions and then, finally, lovers. She had thought Morgan knew her inside and out. But then, Lauren had thought she knew *him* inside and out, too. She'd thought that he loved her, that he'd wanted to marry her.

Lauren had been very wrong about that, and now Morgan was very wrong about her. She had to try again, she decided, whipping the cake batter with unnecessary force. Tonight, after supper, she'd drive over to his house and tell him exactly how it was, whether he wanted to hear it or not. Sooner or later Morgan would put two and two together, and she wanted to tell him before he discovered the truth himself.

* * *

It had already grown dark by the time Lauren drove back out to the highway and headed south. Morgan lived only three miles away.

Before Lauren had left the house she'd changed into a straight skirt of black twill that buttoned up the front and a oversize white shirt. She'd brushed her hair into a cloud of black curls and glossed a shiny plum color across her lips. On the outside she looked cool and beautiful, but on the inside her stomach was in quivering knots. Several times she took deep, calming breaths, but she still felt herself shaking.

There were two houses on the Sinclair place—one huge main house and one guest house, both made of red brick. Even before Lauren had left for Houston, Morgan had made the guest house his home. It was several hundred yards away from the main house, which gave him a large measure of privacy. Perhaps, since his father had passed on, he had moved back into the main house with his mother.

She braked at the guest house and decided to look for him there first. Two huge sycamores towered over most of the front lawn. Lauren noticed that someone had carefully raked the fallen leaves from the sidewalk and left them to one side in several uneven mounds. A few roses were still blooming in the beds next to the house. Apparently the overhang of the porch had sheltered them from this morning's frost.

The heels of her black flats seemed to clatter as she stepped up onto the stone porch. Quickly, before she could change her mind, she pushed the doorbell.

It seemed like an eternity before Lauren heard any

kind of movement inside the house. And even then it was a long time before the porchlight was flipped on and the door opened.

Morgan stood across the threshold from her. There was no mistaking the stunned look on his face. He was dressed in a long-sleeved shirt of maroon and gray stripes and a pair of tight-fitting jeans. His hair looked damp, as if he'd just come out of the shower. "Lauren?"

"I—I'm sorry I left so abruptly today at lunch," she said, smiling faintly and nervously pushing a hand through her hair. "Do you think we might talk a few minutes?"

"Lauren, I…"

"I know I should have called first," she added hastily. "If you're tied up with something, that's all right—"

He suddenly looked uncomfortable. "It's not that I'm tied up. But I'm expected to meet someone in a few minutes."

Lauren didn't have to be told that the someone was a woman. In fact, it didn't really surprise her to learn that his life included the opposite sex. What did surprise her was how much it hurt.

Tight-lipped, Lauren turned away, saying, "Sorry, I didn't mean to interrupt your evening."

Tears blinded her as she hurried down the sidewalk to her car. She blinked them away furiously. Suddenly Morgan's hand closed over hers, and the touch seared right through her. She turned and looked up at him, totally unaware that her eyes looked wide and wounded.

"You don't have to leave," he said. "I have a few minutes—"

A few minutes, she thought bitterly. She'd borne this man's child, and now all he could give her was a few minutes! She looked at him and thought about all the happiness they'd shared in the past. It broke her heart to think that they'd never share their son as real parents, as a real family.

"It's obvious my showing up here was the wrong thing to do," she said, unable to keep the dryness from her voice.

He moved his hand away from hers, but his eyes still held her firmly in their grip. "Why did you?"

She swallowed and asked herself the same ridiculous question, then blurted out, "Because—because I wanted to make a nuisance of myself. That's what I always did where you were concerned, isn't it?"

His features grew hard. "That's a stupid thing to say. Is that what living in the city has done to you? Turned you into a cynic?"

No, not the city, Morgan. You did it to me. Didn't you know? She said bravely, "I've learned many things since I left Mena. This hillbilly heart of mine learned it had to harden up or it couldn't survive in the real world."

Regret slashed through him. He couldn't bear to think that her softness, her gentle and loving heart, had ceased to exist.

"Maybe you've been living in the wrong world," he suggested.

"Not all of us are as fortunate as the Sinclairs. We're not all in a position to pick and choose."

His brows lifted at her caustic words. "Am I supposed to feel guilty for having money?"

"No. But you should feel guilty for judging those who don't."

"Oh, come on, Lauren. You didn't show up here tonight to lecture me."

"I shouldn't have shown up here tonight, period," she muttered. For the second time today, she realized how stupid and foolish she was to think Morgan might want to know about Scott. He had a life far above hers, far away from hers. His social life would hardly leave him time for a child, and Scott certainly didn't need a playboy father.

She turned to go, but his voice made her hesitate. "Lauren, please. Will you come back later?"

She looked back to see that he'd followed her down the sidewalk.

She couldn't believe how just that soft, pleading light in his eyes made her want to throw caution to the winds. "I—I don't think so, Morgan. It wasn't important anyway."

Without bothering to say goodbye, she opened the car door and slipped behind the steering wheel. She could feel Morgan's eyes boring into her as she reversed the car and drove away. But when she turned and headed toward home she didn't look back. This time she was determined never to look back.

Chapter Three

It was still early when Morgan returned home from his date with Angela. After Lauren had surprised him with her appearance at his front door, he hadn't wanted to go on the date, but he'd forced himself to anyway.

Canceling at the last moment would have been treating Angela shabbily. So he'd gone and had struggled to appear normal and attentive. Yet he could hardly remember anything they'd talked about. His mind had been on Lauren the whole time. In fact, it still was.

He lit a cigarette as he headed into the den. He made his way to the wet bar and splashed a considerable amount of Scotch into a squat tumbler.

Morgan rarely drank, even socially, but tonight he felt the urgent need for a swift kick of something.

Seeing Lauren again had left him feeling that the ceiling was about to cave in on him.

Carrying his drink over to an armchair, he sank down on the cushion and let his head fall wearily against the backrest.

Morgan had often thought about Lauren returning to Mena. In fact, he'd counted on her returning to him someday. He'd even imagined how it would be, what he would say to her and how she would look and react. None of it had been the way he'd imagined it.

She had a son! She'd given birth to some other man's child! That fact clawed at his insides. For so long he'd thought that someday they would be together. He'd thought Lauren wanted that, too.

But obviously she didn't. "Of course she didn't, you damn idiot," he muttered to himself, then swallowed a large part of the Scotch.

You told her to go. You told her she was too young for you. You told her she deserved to see more than just the woods in the Arkansas mountains before she settled down with a man.

And why did you tell her that? he asked himself, gulping down the last of the expensive whiskey. Because you made love to her and you felt guilty as hell about it.

Guilty? Hell, yes! She'd given him her love, her innocence, with such blind trust. For two years he'd watched her grow from an awkward seventeen-year-old into a beautiful woman. And somewhere along the way he'd fallen in love with her.

Morgan got up from the armchair and went to refill his glass with Scotch. Looking at the amount remaining in the bottle, he wondered if there was enough left to cloud his mind, to block out the memories charging at him from all directions.

Getting drunk wouldn't help matters, he realized. He jammed the bottle back under the counter and set aside the empty glass.

Morgan couldn't figure out why Lauren had come to his house tonight. She'd seemed very cool and distant when he'd seen her at lunch. But tonight, when he'd first answered the door, she'd been friendly enough until she'd discovered he had a date. None of it made any sense to Morgan, and he wished he could talk to her.

The thought made him look at the telephone and wonder if it would do any good to call her. Would she even agree to talk to him? A glance at his watch told him it was too late to be calling the Magee house.

He'd have to wait until morning, he realized. He'd stop by on his way to work and force her to talk to him if he had to. He had to know why she'd turned to another man.

Damn it, man, what did you expect? You pushed her away. Did you think she'd live like a nun until she finally decided to come home?

The questions deserved another swallow of eighty-proof painkiller, but he ignored the urge and lit a cigarette instead.

Tossing the match in an ashtray, he walked across to the windows at the end of the richly furnished room. The heavy drapes were pulled open to allow a view of the mountains.

The night was clear and lit by a thousand stars. Across the rise to the south of him was the Sinclair Lumber Mill. That was where he'd seen Lauren for the first time. She'd been seventeen then, with a shiny black ponytail, a sprinkling of freckles and a sassy mouth.

Somehow she'd talked his father into letting her carry slabs—or "buck slabs" in mill talk—for the summer. That was before the mill was mechanized and the excess bark and trimmings ripped away by the big circular saws still had to be carried away by hand.

Morgan had walked up on this tiny little thing, in a pair of faded overalls and a red T-shirt, carrying a load of pine that weighed more than half of what she did. Resin was smeared across the bib of her overalls, her cheeks and chin and even the tip of her nose. The rough bark had scratched the insides of her bare arms until the skin was merely a network of raw welts and cuts.

He'd lifted half the slabs from her arms and told her not to carry that many at one time. Then he'd gotten her a long-sleeved shirt from the tool shack. She'd put it on, looking at him all the while as if he were some gallant knight instead of a cocky young college graduate.

At that time, Morgan had just come home from LSU, thinking he was ready to conquer the world and the family lumber business.

His father had quickly taken the vinegar out of him, saying Morgan was going to learn about milling just like everyone else did—from the bottom up. And, to Morgan's chagrin, he'd put him to work bucking slabs along with Lauren.

Morgan's mouth twisted wryly as he remembered how he'd thought his life was ruined. The hours at the mill had been long, the work tiresome and sweaty. Yet it had turned out to be one of the best summers of his life. Thanks to Lauren.

She'd been spunky and hardworking, completely unlike all the other girls he'd known. He'd liked to tease her because she never got angry and was always able to stand her ground with him. And he'd admired her greatly for her determination to work at such a gritty job just to be able to help her mother make a go of things.

It had taken very little time for Morgan to realize that Lauren had a crush on him. At first he'd found it amusing. Then, later, he'd decided it felt pretty good to be worshiped by someone. It had even made him feel important, and it had made him feel responsible for her.

Consequently, he'd taken her under his wing, taught her how to shoot a rifle, how to hunt, how to swim, how to drive a car. He'd even bought her a hunting dog—a black Lab named Jeff. Lauren had been as wild over that dog as most girls would have been over a diamond ring, he thought with a wry twist to his mouth.

Morgan stepped away from the window. He didn't

like the way his mind kept insisting on going over the past. He crossed the room purposefully and switched on the television set. It took only two minutes for Morgan to decide nothing on the screen would be able to distract him from his thoughts about Lauren. He left it on anyway. At least the noise made the house seem not so empty.

By the time he'd finished his cigarette he'd decided it was fruitless to try to keep Lauren's image from floating in front of his eyes. He didn't even try to stop it when the old memory wheel cranked up again.

He remembered how he'd gotten a lot of ribbing from his friends because he and Lauren were good friends. But Morgan hadn't really minded. He'd known many girls when he'd been in college and had even seriously dated one or two. But none of them had really been a soul mate. He hadn't known anyone who could make him laugh, who could make him feel as special and important as Lauren did. He could talk to her about any kind of problem and she'd sit quietly and listen, her big green eyes intent upon him and what he was saying. And then she'd always floor him with some simple, logical solution that had never even crossed his mind.

But then his friend had begun to mature into a young woman. He'd tried to ignore it, but it had been difficult when Lauren's curvy body constantly reminded him.

It was then that he'd realized he'd have to let her go. She'd needed more than just being with him, and he'd told her so.

She had laughed and said, "Morgan, we both know I'm gonna marry you someday. So why should I pretend to like some pimply-faced guy who doesn't know nothin' about nothin'?"

"Oh, you're gonna marry me," he said with a grin. "And you think I know everything about everything."

She smiled endearingly up at him. "Of course. I knew that the first time I saw you."

Damn it, he thought. Why hadn't he ever been able to resist her, especially that night they'd made love?

Because you wanted her for a long time, he told himself. *Because she wanted you, and because making love to her seemed very right, very beautiful. Because you loved her with every fiber of your being.*

But afterward it hadn't seemed that way. All Morgan could think of was how young and innocent she was and how much he'd taken from her. Not just physically, but also emotionally. It hadn't helped his conscience to tell himself that she had wanted him with an equal passion, that she loved him and therefore trusted him utterly.

All those reasons had only served to make him feel like an even bigger heel. He'd succumbed to his desires instead of being a responsible man. When Morgan had seen her the next day, he'd told her he didn't want to see her anymore.

Morgan knew that for as long as he lived, he would never forget the crushed look on her face when she'd whispered, "But you and I—we're gonna get married. Especially now that—"

"You're too young to get married," he'd muttered ruefully, unable to watch the pain fill her eyes.

"I'm nineteen!"

His mouth had twisted. "That's too young. You don't even know what life is all about yet!"

The words had left a stricken look on her face. "I see," she'd choked out painfully. "I was old enough to—to make love, but I'm not old enough to get married."

He'd winced painfully at her reasoning. "Anybody can do what we did last night! But it takes a lot more than jumping into bed with someone to be able to enter a relationship like marriage and make it work."

She'd looked straight into his eyes for what seemed like an eternity. Then suddenly, her chin had dropped. Her voice had quivered when she'd said, "I guess I've had things figured wrong for a long time, haven't I?"

He'd sighed heavily, wondering how he could possibly make her understand how he felt. "Lauren, listen to me. I've always wanted what was best for you. You need to grow up, do and see things before you tie yourself down to marriage."

She'd lifted her face to him, tears sparkling in her eyes. "Then—then we won't get married. That doesn't mean we can't see each other. Please, Morgan!" She'd reached out and touched the spot over his heart. Her hand had appeared tiny and vulnerable against his broad chest. "We've always been together and—and last night you wanted me. I know you did!"

"Of course I wanted you!" he'd snapped out of

sheer helplessness. ''I still want you! That's the whole problem. We can't change our relationship back to what it was, and we damn sure aren't going to repeat last night!''

''But—''

''Look, Lauren, I'm trying to be selfless about this. So go home, or go anyplace away from me! I'm a grown man, for God's sake, and you're just getting out of high school! Give yourself time to grow up and enjoy this young, precious time. You can always come back after a while—and when you do you're going to thank me for this.''

Lauren hadn't said anything then. She'd burst into tears and run from him. Morgan had watched her go, pain and remorse twisting his heart.

That was the last time he'd seen her. A few days later, her mother had told him that she had gone to Houston.

He'd been relieved at the time, because he'd known that if she stayed he would wind up making love to her again. But it had been only a few days before Morgan was missing her like hell. It had been a constant struggle for him not to go to her mother and ask for Lauren's address. The decent side of him battled with the emptiness in his heart. In the end, both choices had made him feel like a loser. And now, after all these years, he felt like an even bigger loser.

Now all Morgan could think of was that Lauren had been hurt, first by him, and obviously again by some other man. He'd never intended for that to happen. She'd always been so precious to him, and he'd wanted her to have all the good things she deserved. She hadn't deserved bearing and raising a child on her own. Why had it happened?

Well into the cold morning hours, Morgan was still trying to find the answers.

Lauren was just getting out of the shower when she heard a knock on the door. Without bothering to dry off, she wrapped the white chenille robe around her and hurried out of the bathroom.

A tangled wet mass of curls danced in front of her eyes. One hand reached up to rake it back while the other reached for the door knob.

Lauren froze when she opened the door and saw Morgan standing on the wooden porch. He was dressed in jeans, a khaki shirt and a pair of maize-colored cowboy boots. He looked big and vital and very masculine. But he also looked haggard and his eyes were bloodshot, as if he hadn't slept at all last night.

Apparently the date had kept him busy, Lauren thought. Then she did her best to push the idea out of her mind. "What do you want?"

His mouth cocked upward at her blunt greeting. "Can't you say, 'Good morning, Morgan'?"

"Sorry, I'm not feeling very civil this morning," she said honestly. She'd stayed awake at least half the night berating herself for ever having driven over to Morgan's in the first place.

"Then how about, 'Come in'?" he countered with a disarming grin.

A part of her wanted to refuse him. A part of her wanted to slam the door in his face. But there was still a big part of her that melted, turned as soft as butter, at the sight of him.

She had loved him so deeply, had centered her world around him for so long, that not even the past four years of pain could wipe away the sweetness of seeing him again.

Reluctantly she moved aside and pushed the door wide, allowing Morgan to step into the house.

Lauren had built up a roaring fire before she'd gotten into the shower. Without looking at Morgan, she crossed to it and stood close to the flames. The dampness of the shower left her chilled and shaking, but not nearly as much as Morgan's presence did.

"I suppose you're on the way to the mill."

It was spoken as a statement, but he answered just the same. "Yes."

"How is it doing these days?" she asked, having decided that it would be much safer to bring up something impersonal. "I've heard building contracts are down now."

His eyes on Lauren, he walked farther into the room. The white material of her robe clung to her in a soft, provocative way. She'd always been petite. Strangely, she appeared even smaller now than he remembered, or maybe the vulnerable aura about her only made her seem that way.

Lauren lifted her arm and pushed the wet hair away from her face. The movement drew his attention to her breasts. They were very small, too, but firm and perfectly shaped. Morgan wondered whether, if he pushed the material of her robe aside, he would find the petal-pink nipples rigid and waiting.

"I haven't felt the crunch," he said. "But then, I ship my lumber hundreds of miles out. That makes a big difference."

"Yes, I guess it would," she replied, and hugged her arms around her waist in an unconscious gesture of defensiveness at his presence. "Mother said there's been a big controversy over logging here in the Ouachita, between the hunters, the conservationists and the timber industry."

Morgan's mouth curved knowingly. It was obvious to him that Lauren was deliberately steering the conversation away from any uncomfortable subjects. "Eileen is right. It's still going on, in fact."

"And which side are you on?" she asked.

He jammed his hands in the front pockets of his jeans. "I don't believe in clear-cutting, even though I'm a timberman. It strips the forest's natural habitat, and I believe there are some things that should always be cherished and protected."

That comment didn't surprise Lauren. In a way, he'd had the same feelings about her. Down through the years Morgan had always wanted to shelter her, as though she were some innocent child, still too young and fragile to be let out in the world. In the past years, while Lauren had been away from him, she had often wondered if he'd ever considered her grown-up. He'd made love to her. But then, he'd also told her that anyone could do that. Those words still had the power to infuriate her, to tear at her heart. Maybe any woman could make love to Morgan and it would be the same for him. But it could never be that way for Lauren.

Lauren could feel his eyes on her. She shifted restlessly and thrust her palms toward the crackling flames. "Sorry about last night, Morgan," she said curtly. "I was imposing. I should have called first."

After Lauren had thought about the whole incident, she'd been very embarrassed and very angry at herself. She'd acted jealous when she had no reason or right to. There was no telling how Morgan had construed her strange behavior.

Morgan shrugged, wondering how they could be so impersonal with each other when they'd been so close for so long. "I'm sorry, too."

His apology caught her off guard. Looking away, she took a deep breath. "I don't suppose you came by to talk timber."

"No."

Lauren turned slowly toward him. "Then why did you?"

"To find out why you came to see me last night."

Suddenly Lauren felt her heart reacting to the fear rushing through her. She'd tossed and turned, wondered and debated over and over whether to go through with her plan to tell Morgan that Scott was his son. She still couldn't decide whether it would be the right thing, the best thing to do. And now, at this moment? No! She needed more space, more time to feel Morgan out, to search for that part of him she'd loved so desperately.

Lauren shrugged, affecting an air of nonchalance that hurt both him and her. Her voice husky, she said, "It's been a long time since I've been home, Morgan. I thought—I just thought we might visit for a bit."

He squinted at her lowered face. "Is that all? I had the impression you came for a specific reason."

She looked up, not realizing how pale she'd grown. "Well, you're wrong. Besides, what possible reason would I have, other than the one I just told you?"

He frowned impatiently and reached for a cigarette. While he lit it, Lauren glanced toward the hallway. Scott would be waking at any moment. She didn't want him to appear while Morgan was still here. She didn't want Morgan to have the opportunity to study her son. There was always that chance he might pick up on some familiar characteristic and put two and two together.

"That's what I'm here to find out," Morgan answered.

"Sorry," she said, forcing a light smile to her lips. "That's all there was to it. I hope I didn't ruin your date."

He frowned. Thanks to her, it was difficult to remember that he'd even had a date. "You didn't."

Lauren's brows lifted, but she didn't speak. She was thinking that maybe at his age he skipped the formality of dating and went straight to the main event. The thought made her grind her teeth.

"Look, Morgan," she said suddenly, making an

effort to wrap the robe closer around her, "I've just gotten out of the shower, and I need to dress. Maybe we could do this some other time."

He smiled, but there was nothing nice about his expression. "I know where the kitchen is. I'll drink some coffee while you dress."

His unexpected determination threw Lauren off balance. She'd figured he'd said all he'd wanted to say to her yesterday in town. And last night? Last night he'd been on his way to see another woman. A grand time to let him know he was a father!

"I... Won't your workers be expecting the boss to show?"

The twisted smile on his face deepened. "Trying to get rid of me, Lauren? You know, your behavior seems very mixed up. First you say you want to talk. Now I'm giving you the chance and you don't want it."

She laughed to cover her nervousness. It sounded dry and forced, even to her own ears. "Well, I guess I always was mixed up where you were concerned, Morgan."

Morgan went still. Then suddenly came to life, crossing the room with eyes that glittered angrily.

Lauren took a bracing stance and looked up into his face as he halted mere inches from her.

"I think you have it all wrong," he said in soft, dangerous tones. "I believe *I* was the one who got things all mixed up—about you."

Down through the years, Lauren had often imagined how it would be to confront Morgan face-to-face.

As the weeks away from Mena had turned into months and then into years, the things she'd planned to say to him had changed, but the purpose behind them had not. And that purpose was to wound him, to hurt him as badly as he had hurt her.

Funny how difficult it was at this moment for her to concentrate on revenge. She hadn't counted on Morgan's nearness being so overwhelming. She hadn't prepared herself for this sudden assault of memories so sharp and sweet that her throat ached with tears.

"You haven't married," she blurted out huskily before she could stop herself.

Even though his brown eyes were bloodshot, they still had a cold, piercing effect. Lauren wondered how such an icy look could make her feel hot and suffused with color.

"Should I have wanted to be?" he countered.

Lauren moistened her lips, and would have stepped away from him, but the fireplace blocked her from behind. She suddenly felt surrounded by flames. "Most men do marry—eventually," she drawled. "When they find the right person." Obviously that person hadn't been Lauren. He'd made that quite plain.

His nostrils flared, and she could feel his eyes sliding away from her face, down over her throat and settling on the creamy vee between her breasts. The look in his eyes made her feel exposed, in more ways than one. And she wondered if he remembered what it had been like to touch her there. Did he know she could still feel the hard line of his lips upon her, the warm imprint of his hands?

"Apparently *you* didn't find the right person," he said.

Lauren supposed he meant Scott's father. God, wasn't that laughable! she thought hysterically. Shaking her head, she said quietly, almost sadly, "No, I didn't."

Morgan moved closer, and for one crazy moment Lauren thought he was going to reach out and touch her. He was so close now that she could see the pores in his tanned skin, the tiny lines at his eyes and around his mouth, the way the sun kissed the tips of his unruly curls.

He was young, sexy, successful and heartless. Lauren kept reminding herself of that last trait over and over again. It was something she couldn't ever afford to forget.

"You never wrote. You never called. You never came back," he said.

His low voice was filled with accusation. Lauren was stunned. What had this man expected? What did he expect from her now?

She tried to laugh, but it came out more like a whimper. "I learned my lesson well, Morgan. I should have," she added. "You drilled it into me well enough."

"Lesson?"

Her heart was pounding with anger and fear—and with something else, something that was reckless and heady and made her want to throw herself into his arms. Inside, she was shaking violently. Outwardly, her fingers trembled. She thrust them out of sight beneath the folds of her robe. "About making myself scarce when I'm not wanted," she told him.

His features were as hard as stone. "You didn't understand then, any more than you understand now," he said tightly.

"I was naive then. I didn't understand a lot of things. And maybe I'm still naive, but I do understand. Now that I've been away, grown up and seen how things really are," she said bitterly.

His eyes roamed her face as if he were searching for answers but could not find them. "And what do you see, Lauren?"

For the life of her, Lauren couldn't figure out why he was asking, why he even cared to know what she thought. "I see how it is with people like me and you. I was a loser before anything ever started between us. But then, you knew that, didn't you, Morgan? You knew that all along. You just didn't have the gumption to tell me. No, instead you wanted to lead me on, make me believe I meant something to you, that sometimes people like us could live together happily ever after. I've often wondered just how many good laughs you've had behind my back."

She was angry now and close to losing control. Tears stung her eyes but, determined not to let him see the power he still had to hurt her, she blinked them back.

"You bitter little fool," he exclaimed, reaching for her shoulders and giving her a hard shake. "You have no idea how it was with me! You don't even want to try to find out.''

"I know enough," she said through clenched teeth. "I know that you stomped all over my heart. That after I left Mena you never once tried to contact me!"

His grip on her shoulders eased, but she was hardly aware of it. She could only stare into his eyes, wondering why, after all the pain he'd caused her, she still wanted to feel his lips on hers, to feel his arms around her, comforting her, loving her, showing her the passion she had yet to find anywhere else.

"Did you want me to contact you?"

For a moment Lauren stared at him in amazement. Then her eyes dropped away from his face. Did she want him to? My God, how could he not know, not feel, all the hours and days she'd ached for him? How could he not know how she'd yearned for him all through the months she'd carried his child inside her? And how could he not know that when she'd lain in the hospital in labor it was his name she'd cried out, him she'd wanted by her side to help her bear the pain and share the joy of bearing their child?

Lauren's eyes lifted back to him and a part of her turned cold. No, he didn't know, she thought. And he didn't care. She had gone through it all alone. She was raising her son alone. He had forced her to make that decision.

Morgan had crushed her pride when he'd turned his back on her. She was determined to hold on to what little of it she had left. She said, "I admit that I made a fool of myself over you, Morgan. And for a while I did want to hear from you. But I finally got over my infatuation with you. So you can breathe easy. I didn't come back to Mena to chase you like a lovesick teenager."

Desperately Lauren shrugged away from his grasp and tried to step around him.

His fingers closed roughly around her wrist, halting her. "Damn it," he growled. "Why are you acting this way? Why do you hate me, when all I ever did was love you?"

Incredulous, she stared at him. "Oh, that is rich, Morgan! Really rich!"

"I want to know, Lauren. I want to know why you stayed away, why you had another man's child."

With one sudden jerk she tore her wrist from his grasp. "That, Morgan, is none of your business!"

"I'm making it my business," he said, following close on her heels as she stalked toward the kitchen.

"It's too late for that," she threw over her shoulder.

Once in the kitchen, Lauren reached blindly for a coffee cup—not because she wanted coffee, but because she had to do something, anything, to interrupt the chain of thoughts running through her mind. She was afraid that if Morgan made her angry enough she might blurt out something she would regret for the rest of her life.

"You think you know so much," he said. "You think because you've gone away and lived in a big city you know it all. You don't know a damn thing!"

Fury raged through her. She knew plenty. She

knew about loneliness, about shame, about humiliation. She knew about the worry and fear of supporting herself and her child. He was the one who knew nothing!

Hold on to yourself, Lauren, a voice inside her cautioned. *Don't lose control! Don't tell him now! Not when he's angry and blaming you. And not when you're angry and blaming him.*

"I know I want you to leave," she said to him, her voice hoarse.

Before she realized his intentions, Morgan closed the gap between them and pinned her against the cabinets. The breath rushed from Lauren at their sudden, unexpected contact.

"I won't go until you do some explaining," he said. "Not until you tell me why I never heard from you until yesterday. Why you had another man's child!"

Lauren's mouth dropped open. She felt on fire where his body touched hers, but her face and hands felt oddly cold and clammy. *My God, what am I going to do?* she wondered wildly. She couldn't lie to him, but she couldn't tell him the truth, either.

"Morgan, I—"

"Mama?"

Both of them turned instantly to see Scott standing just inside the kitchen door. The boy's dark green eyes were wide and bright, and he was studying Morgan with childlike curiosity.

"Are you my daddy?" he asked.

Chapter Four

Lauren was so stunned by Scott's untimely question that she could only stare helplessly at the both of them.

Morgan was the first one to break the tense silence. Pushing away from Lauren, he crossed the small space to Scott and knelt down to the boy's level.

"Haven't you ever seen your daddy?" Morgan asked gently.

Scott slowly measured the big man in front of him, then bashfully shook his head in answer.

The response made Morgan turn a cold, accusing glare on Lauren. She cringed inwardly at the sight of it. Then feeling the need to defend herself, she opened her mouth, only to find there was nothing she could say. How could she possibly defend herself without letting out the truth?

Morgan looked at Scott again, and his harsh expression softened. Precious innocence stared back at him. Morgan couldn't imagine any man not acknowledging this child. "Why do you think I might be your daddy?" he asked carefully.

Scott stuck his finger in his mouth, then pulled it out and cocked his head to one side. "'Cause Mama said we'd have to go a long ways to see my daddy. And yesterday we went a long ways."

"I see," Morgan said. He smiled at the child. "Well, I think this time your mama came a long way so you could see your grandma."

Scott nodded as though he understood, and Morgan rose. Lauren's heart was thudding heavily when he turned back to her. She desperately hoped he believed that seeing Eileen was the only reason she'd brought Scott all the way to Mena.

As Morgan took in Lauren's pale features, her guarded expression, he felt both angry and disappointed. It was sad for him to realize that her son did not know his own father, and he hated to think that Lauren had been so irresponsible.

Even so, he had to remind himself that lots of time had passed since he'd last seen Lauren. He didn't know what had gone on in her life. She didn't know what had gone on in his. There had to be an explanation to all this, he told himself. He couldn't imagine that Lauren had changed so much from the young woman he'd known.

The anger drained from his face as he moved away from Scott and back to Lauren. "Lauren, I never thought—I never imagined it would be like this when you came back to Mena."

There was no accusation in his words. Instead, Lauren found a hint of concern and regret running through his deep voice. The sound of both emotions took her completely off guard. There had been a time in her life when she'd believed there wasn't a more compassionate man in the world than Morgan. Was it possible that there was still a bit of that compassion in him?

Her eyes slanted away from his and fixed themselves on the shiny linoleum floor. "Neither did I, Morgan. I guess—I guess it's like they say, we never know what lies ahead for any of us."

Lauren's voice was tinged with sadness, and suddenly Morgan realized just how much she must have gone through over the four years they'd been apart. It couldn't have been easy, bearing and raising a child without a father. "That's true," he said.

Scott spoke up, breaking the awkward tension. "Mama, I'm hungry."

Lauren looked at her son. "Mama's hungry, too," she told him. "Would you like eggs or pancakes this morning?"

"Pancakes!" he shouted happily.

"Then run to the bathroom and wash your hands while Mama starts cooking."

His short, sturdy little legs carried him out of the room in a hurry. Lauren's eyes followed Scott until he was beyond the door. Then she forced herself to meet Morgan's gaze.

"He's a beautiful little boy," he said.

And he's yours, she wanted to say. But, of course, the words wouldn't come. She knew that when she admitted the truth about Scott's father, an explosion was sure to follow. She wasn't ready to face that just yet.

Taking a deep breath, she turned to the refrigerator and began taking out eggs and milk. "Thank you, Morgan. I'm very proud of him."

Morgan watched her set the food on the counter. She then took down a mixing bowl from its shelf.

"You should be."

She glanced over her shoulder at him. "That surprises me, coming from you, Morgan."

He shrugged and moved a few steps closer. "Why?"

Lauren swallowed and fought the urge to close her eyes. His nearness and the secret that hung between them were making a mess of her composure. "Yesterday you seemed to think my having Scott was something dirty."

He frowned impatiently. "Yesterday it was a shock for me to find you back here in Mena, much less find you with a child. I didn't have time to form any kind of opinion about it one way or the other."

"I think you're lying about that, Morgan. But if you think labeling me as loose will make me regret having Scott, you couldn't be more wrong. He's everything in my life, and I've never wished I could turn back time or change the fact that he was conceived."

Something twisted painfully inside Morgan as he weighed her words. Apparently she had loved the father very much, for it was obvious she didn't regret having his child.

She used to vow her love to him. Morgan wondered how long it had taken for that love to fade.

Before Morgan could reply, Lauren turned back to her work at the counter. She could hear the water running in the bathroom and knew that Scott was probably having a high old time playing with it and the pump bottle of soap. The room would be a shambles. But then, so would she if Morgan didn't leave soon.

"I didn't mean to imply that you should be ashamed of having a child," he told her.

"I'm not," she said with swift conviction.

He sighed and thrust his hand through his curly hair. "Look, Lauren, I know we somehow managed to get off on the wrong foot—"

"I made the mistake of thinking you might want to—to talk. I imposed on your privacy. But, like I said, it won't happen again." Lauren's throat ached, and she marveled that her voice didn't show it.

"Damn it, Lauren."

The words were a whispered string of regret. Lauren looked up at him with startled, questioning eyes.

Morgan stepped closer, then reached out and curved his hand over her shoulder. Touching her was like falling back in time, he thought, as painful memories rushed through him.

"Did you expect me to be indifferent to seeing you again, and with a child?"

She took a deep breath, then allowed her gaze to fall to the large brown fingers on her shoulder. "I really didn't know," she said honestly.

He muttered something to himself that made Lauren lift her eyes to his again. "Does it really matter what I expected, Morgan?"

He suddenly felt so frustrated by it all that he had to stifle the urge to shout, "Hell, yes." But he knew that arguing, shouting and accusing wouldn't change a thing. And the one thing that he could pull out of the turmoil inside him was that he didn't want Lauren to feel bitter toward him.

"Yes, it matters to me, Lauren."

Something in his voice made her believe him, even though she knew it was unwise to do so. "It's been so long," she whispered. "I—I'd come to hope that maybe we could put the past behind us. That maybe we could still be friends."

The tension drained out of him, and his fingers loosened and began moving gently against her shoulder. "Somehow I don't think we could ever be just 'friends.' But I would like to put the past behind us."

Lauren swallowed nervously and stepped away from him. She had to. She couldn't keep looking into his face and still hold herself together. "We had many good times together, Morgan."

He watched her as she awkwardly began to spoon flour into a measuring cup. "Yes, we did," he said.

"And I would like to talk with you, Lauren. Will you let me take you out to dinner tonight?"

The spoon in her hand stopped halfway to the bowl, but she didn't turn and look at him. She didn't trust herself to.

"Do you really want to, Morgan? Or do you just feel compelled to make the gesture?"

Morgan studied the set of her small shoulders and the black curls lying against them. Even though she outwardly resembled the Lauren he'd known, inwardly she was nothing like her. That fact hit him hard.

"I really want to."

Tense moments passed before Lauren found the courage to turn and face him. Somehow she had to appear cool and controlled. She couldn't let him see that all her old feelings for him were still there, still bottled up tightly in her heart.

"Then I'd be glad to accept your invitation. What time shall I look for you?"

"How about six-thirty?"

"Fine."

"Lauren—"

"Look, Mama! Look at my hands. I got them real clean!"

Scott's sudden, rambunctious appearance broke the moment between the two adults.

Lauren bent down to inspect her son's hands, wondering as she did what Morgan had been about to say to her.

"That looks great, honey," she told Scott. "Now

climb up in one of the chairs at the table and be a good boy while I finish breakfast.''

Scott scrambled quickly into one of the wooden chairs, and Lauren poured him a small glass of orange juice to satisfy him until the food was prepared.

"Would you like to stay for breakfast, Morgan?'' she forced herself to ask. He'd met her halfway, or so it seemed, with the dinner invitation. It would appear unhospitable not to offer to share their meal with him.

"Thank you, Lauren. But I'm expected at the mill shortly.'' He was very surprised that she'd asked him. It also made him uneasy when it dawned on him just how much he'd like to stay here in this warm kitchen with this woman and her child. Whatever he'd expected from seeing her again, it hadn't been the warm hunger inside him now.

Relief and regret pushed and pulled at Lauren as she watched Morgan head toward the door that lead out to the backyard.

He turned to look at her just as he was about to step over the threshold. "I'll see you this evening,'' he told Lauren. Then, he looked at Scott, who was still seated obediently at the table. "'Bye, boy.''

Scott giggled bashfully, then said, "'Bye.''

With a wry smile, Morgan shut the door behind him. Lauren sank weakly against the kitchen cabinets. Dear God, would she ever have come back if she'd known how hard all this was going to be?

One look at Scott's innocent face reminded her that the answer to that question had to be yes.

* * *

"Are you sure about this, Lauren?" her mother asked later that evening as she watched her daughter dress for dinner with Morgan.

Lauren was sitting on the side of the bed, pulling on a pair of sheer stockings. She looked at her mother, who sat perched on a dressing stool, no more than an arm's length away.

"Do you mean my going out with Morgan, or my telling him about Scott?"

Eileen sighed and shook her head. "Both, I suppose."

Lauren stood and allowed the dress she'd pulled over her head to fall down her hips and swirl around her calves. It was soft cotton knit in pale pink with a dropped waist and long sleeves. The dress wasn't exactly a winter garment, but since it had long sleeves, she was making do with it.

"Morgan is a good man, but that doesn't mean he's going to take any of this lying down."

Stepping into her low-heeled pumps, Lauren asked, "What do you mean by that?"

Eileen frowned. "Just what I said. I have a feeling that if he discovers he's Scott's father he'll demand his parental rights."

Lauren shook her head. "I really doubt it, Mother. I don't think he'll want to be bothered with such a responsibility. After all, he obviously didn't want to be bothered with me."

"Lauren, that isn't so!"

Lauren pursed her lips as she walked over to the

dressing table where her mother sat. "Let's face it, Mother. After he'd gotten what he wanted from me he was no longer interested."

"That's a terrible thing to say! And I don't want to hear you talking that way!"

"Oh, Mom." Lauren groaned dismally. "The last thing I want is to upset you. I don't mean to sound so harsh and bitter. It's just— Well, it's just hard not to after all Morgan put me through."

Eileen gave her daughter a long, pointed look. "Morgan wasn't all to blame. You put yourself through a lot of unnecessary agony."

Lauren began to pull a brush through her thick black hair. "How so?"

"For starters, you refused to include Morgan in Scott's birth or his raising."

Lauren sighed. She and her mother had been over this many times in the past. She saw no use in going over it again. Particularly when Morgan was going to be here in less than twenty minutes and she needed to be in a calm state of mind.

"That is something that can't be undone. And I don't understand how you can sit there and say Morgan is a 'good man.'"

"Morgan *is* a good man." Eileen sighed and rose from the stool. "I just think you were too young to understand Morgan's motives all those years ago. Have you ever stopped to think that *he* might have been hurt, too?"

Lauren turned an amazed look on her mother. "Morgan hurt? Morgan is a Sinclair. He's had everything he ever wanted. I imagine the only time he's ever been hurt was when he lost his father. Getting me out of his hair certainly wouldn't have caused him any grief.''

Eileen shook her head disappointedly and started toward the door. ''Morgan cared for you once, Lauren. Please just try to keep that in mind tonight.''

Lauren's eyes dropped from her image in the mirror. Her mother's words had struck a chord inside her. Yes, she believed Morgan had cared for her at one time, but somewhere along the way he'd changed. But then, Lauren had to admit that she'd changed, too.

Smiling faintly, she looked over at her mother. ''I will remember, Mother. And please don't worry.''

Don't worry. An hour later Lauren was repeating those words to herself as she sat in the front seat of Morgan's car.

They were driving north through the mountains on Highway 71. It had grown dark some time ago, and she could see nothing of the scenery. Lauren doubted she would have enjoyed it even if it had been daylight. She could think of nothing but Morgan—the way he looked, the sound of his voice, and the fact that she was with him again after all these years.

''This is a fairly new place,'' Morgan said. ''I think they built it about two years ago. It's nothing elaborate, but the steak and the seafood are both delicious.''

Lauren looked across at him. ''I'm sure it will be fine,'' she murmured.

Morgan had changed from the boots and jeans he'd been wearing this morning to a pair of dark brown slacks and a white long-sleeved shirt with a faint brown stripe running through it.

She turned her head and stared through the windshield, thinking he looked just as powerful and masculine as she'd always remembered.

Lauren had never met anyone with eyes the color of Morgan's. After she'd gone to Houston she'd often found herself looking at other men, comparing them to Morgan and asking herself what was so different about him. Then she'd realized that he was unique to her simply because she loved him. Still, she'd never encountered another pair of brown eyes exactly like Morgan's. They were a rich, spicy brown, like cinnamon and nutmeg, and they glittered with life, a life she'd once been so much a part of.

"You're very quiet, Lauren. I thought we were going to use this time for a visit?"

Forcing herself to smile, she glanced at him again. "So we were. But I guess I'm afraid to say anything. I don't want us to argue tonight."

To her amazement, he chuckled softly as he steered the luxurious white Lincoln around a sharp mountain curve. "What makes you think we're going to argue? We never used to argue unless it was in fun."

She shrugged. "I know. But that was before—" Before they'd made love and everything had changed. She did her best to shake the thought away. "Well, I'm sorry I've been so defensive, Morgan."

He looked across at her. The gentle curves of her

cheek and lips were illuminated by the dashlights. She was still a very young woman, even though four years had passed. And as he looked at her he realized that the protective way he'd always felt toward her had never left him. "And I'm sorry if I seemed judgmental," he said.

She slanted him a look beneath her black lashes. "Do you really mean that, Morgan?"

The husky sound of her voice made Morgan want to pull over and take her in his arms. "Yes, I do, Lauren. I wouldn't have said it otherwise."

His answer seemed to please her, for she smiled at him and relaxed back against the seat. "How are your mother and your sister doing these days?" she asked.

"Dianne is fine. She married a man from Kentucky last year. He raises thoroughbreds on a thirty-five-hundred-acre farm. I was afraid at first that she was merely dazzled by his wealth and his life-style. But it seems she genuinely loves him, and as it turns out they're very happy."

"That's nice. I take it she doesn't have any children yet."

Morgan shook his head. "I think she wants to enjoy herself a bit more before she settles down to raising a family."

"Yes, children are a big responsibility," she said, but refused to go any further. She didn't want to open herself up to questions about Scott right now. She had two weeks here in Mena, and she wanted to get used to seeing Morgan again before she tackled the job of telling him about Scott.

Morgan sensed her reluctance to mention being a mother herself. He wondered why, especially since she'd gone to such pains to tell him how proud she was of her son. It didn't quite fit, but he would have to respect her privacy. Obviously something hadn't worked out between her and the father. He longed to know, even though the idea of her being with another man cut him like a knife.

"Mother is doing pretty well now," he went on conversationally. "It was very hard on her...losing Dad so suddenly. But, as you know, she's a strong woman, and she has lots of friends who keep her busy with social functions."

Lauren clasped her hands nervously on her lap. "I was truly sorry about your father. He was a delightful man. I'll never forget how kind he was to give me a job at the mill."

Morgan chuckled. "I'll never forget how mad I was at him when he put me to work bucking slabs, too. It was probably one of the best things he ever did for me, though."

She glanced his way. "Why do you say that?"

His mouth curved into a wry smile. "You don't remember how cocky I was back then?"

Lauren smiled and realized her earlier nervousness was draining away. Maybe they could be together without slinging accusations back and forth. "Well, I seem to remember you were pretty confident."

"Hmm. You're being kind now, Lauren. But anyway, it wasn't just because it took me down a notch or two. I also got to know you."

She looked away from him and down at her clasped fingers. "I thought that was something you regretted."

"Is that why you didn't come back?"

It was suddenly a struggle for her to breathe. She wanted to cry and let the tears wash the pain of losing him away. Her fingers gripped each other even tighter. "I didn't come back because there was nothing to come back for," she whispered.

Did she consider him nothing? he wondered. There were so many things he wanted to ask her, but he sensed that tonight was too soon to bring it all up. One thing he did know, however, was that he didn't intend for her to get away again without his knowing how things really stood.

"I thought you considered Mena your home."

"I do. But I can make a much better living in Houston," she told him, relieved when a cluster of lights suddenly appeared up ahead.

Morgan slowed the Lincoln and signalled for the turn. Since it was the first day of the workweek, there were very few cars in front of the restaurant. He parked at one end of the building, then helped Lauren from the car.

The air had already grown very cold, and she shivered beneath the coat she'd borrowed from her mother.

"Are you cold?" Morgan asked, curving his arm around her waist.

His affectionate touch took her by surprise, but she tried not to let him know it. Instead, she nodded and said, "It's been a long time since I've been in cold weather. I guess my system hasn't become acclimatized yet."

"You haven't become a snowbird on me, have you?"

She looked up questioningly to see he was grinning down at her. The sight was very disarming. "Snowbird?"

"You know. Those birds that go south because they can't stand the cold weather."

Lauren shook her head as they passed through the double glass doors. "Not at all. I'm really enjoying the cold weather and the foliage and fires in the fireplace. It seems like a long time since I've gotten to see any of it."

"It has been a long time, Lauren."

Something in Morgan's voice made Lauren look up at him. The smile had vanished from his face, and the amusement had left his brown eyes. Was he actually saying he'd missed her? *No, Lauren,* she told herself. *Don't be fooled all over again by this man.*

There was only a handful of customers sitting in the booths and at the wooden tables inside the restaurant. She and Morgan chose to sit at a booth by the window, and a waitress came to take their order. Morgan asked for a bottle of wine, and they sipped it while they waited for their steaks.

It had been a very long time since Lauren had been out to dinner with anyone, much less a man. She had dated since she'd been in Houston, but she could count those times on the fingers of one hand. She just

hadn't been interested. So why was being here with
Morgan turning out to be so pleasant? Lauren refused
to answer that question, because to think of it reminded her of all she'd lost.

"You know, I'd almost forgotten how beautiful the
mountains are," she mused, her eyes drifting dream-
ily toward the large plate-glass window. "I wish it
were daylight so we could see them now."

He smiled faintly and indulged in the pleasure of
looking at her. He'd pictured Lauren in his mind
every day since she'd gone away. Seeing her again
was feeding the hunger in his heart.

He realized it wasn't a smart thing, but how did a
man stop hungering for a woman? he asked himself.
He hadn't found the answer, and he certainly hadn't
managed to cure himself of her.

"I imagine there are some people who'd feel stifled
living in these mountains," Morgan said, reaching for
his wineglass.

Lauren turned her gaze to him again. He was leaning back casually, with one arm resting across the
back of the booth. The relaxed position had stretched
the cotton shirt across his massive chest. The sight of
it shattered her efforts to look at him as if he were
just another man. Morgan Sinclair was not just another man. That fact was being brought home to her
with a vengeance.

"I never felt stifled. Being in the mountains makes
me feel closer to God, because I know such beauty
couldn't be made without his help," she said.

He took a sip of his wine, then looked at her from

beneath lowered lids. "You're sounding very philo-
sophical."

She smiled, a bit whimsically. "Yes. Well, I guess
being home has done that to me." Lauren lifted her
eyes from the wall of his chest up to his face. Yet
looking at his face wasn't any less distracting to her.
His dark skin and sandy-blond hair were a rich combination. He was golden and brown, rough and manly.
He was—and had been from the moment he'd picked
her up—overwhelming her.

Lauren knew she should have more self-control.
She knew letting herself be charmed by his looks and
his voice was self-destructive. But she had no earthly
idea of how to stop herself.

"How long are you planning on staying?" he
asked suddenly.

She moistened her lips and deliberately looked
away from him. "Two weeks."

"I imagine Eileen wishes it was a month. She
misses you."

He said it as if he knew, as if in some ways he
were closer to her mother than she. It was difficult
for her to think that things here in Mena had gone on
as they always had while her life had changed so
drastically. It made her feel left out and more than a
little sad.

"I don't particularly like living away from Mother.
But you'll learn that children take precedence over
your own wants when you have their welfare to consider."

One golden-brown eyebrow lifted in wry speculation. He repeated her words. "I'll learn. Are you expecting me to have children soon?"

Her heart gave a sudden lurch. He didn't know about Scott. He couldn't. But she knew, and she couldn't meet his gaze. Reaching for her wineglass, she said, "I was merely speaking in general. I have to work hard at what I do, but I do make enough to take care of Scott and myself. I'm not sure I could get that much business here in Mena."

"Scott. That's your son's name?"

She nodded and took another drink of wine.

"He looks like you," Morgan told her.

Every nerve inside her was tightening with dread. Would he have the gall to come right out and ask her who Scott's father was?

"Most people tell me that," she said.

"He doesn't know his father. What happened? Obviously things didn't turn out for you."

Lauren gripped the stem of her glass and silently shouted at herself to remain cool. Shrugging casually she took a deep breath. "I thought he'd made a commitment to me. But it turned out he hadn't," she told him in a raw voice.

He didn't say anything for a long moment, and Lauren found the courage to raise her eyes to his. The compassion in his face took her by swift surprise. She had to fight the urge to cry out that the whole thing was a farce.

"I'm very sorry about that, Lauren," he finally said. "Yet there were other choices you could have made— You could have—"

"Aborted? Put him up for adoption?" she asked, stunned. "God, Morgan, you know me better than that!"

He grimaced and looked down into his wineglass. "Yes. I do know there would be no way you could give up your child. And I admire you for that, Lauren."

The breath she'd been holding rushed from her lungs. "I'd like to think you really mean that, Morgan."

His brown eyes slanted up at her. "I do mean it. But that doesn't mean the hurt has gone away."

The hurt, she repeated to herself. Was he trying to tell her he'd been hurt by all this? To be hurt meant that you cared. Could her mother possibly have been right?

The question had her looking at him with searching eyes. If so, it might change lots of things. Especially the way Morgan would react to learning that Scott was his son.

"Morgan, four years ago, before I went to Houston, I would have believed anything you told me. But now it's hard for me to believe your sincerity. When you pushed me away from you, it was like kicking me in the face. I don't intend to open myself up for another kick."

He shook his head ruefully and set his wineglass to one side. Then, before Lauren could guess his intention, he leaned forward and gathered her hand in his. "That's why I wanted you with me tonight. To let you know that, no matter what, I never meant to hurt you, Lauren.''

His fingers were warm and gentle against hers, a soothing balm to an old, aching wound. She looked in his brown eyes and felt her heart lurch with that old familiar feeling.

Back in Houston, Lauren had resolved to be cool and indifferent toward Morgan. So far she'd managed to do neither. And if she wasn't careful she was going to set herself up for another fall.

"That hardly matters now," she told him now in a quiet voice. "You have your life and I have mine."

He studied her face for a long moment, trying to see what was behind the shadows in her eyes. Her hand was so small and soft in his, and Morgan was suddenly reminded of how she'd once clung to his hand with love and trust. Had all that died? he wondered.

"Lauren, I—"

She looked up to see that the waitress had arrived with their food. Morgan was forced to let go of her hand and lean back so that the waitress could serve them.

Lauren took a deep breath and began to spread her napkin across her lap. The moment between them was over. She'd probably never know what he'd been about to say. And perhaps it was better that way.

Chapter Five

The lights were out in the Magee house when Morgan pulled the Lincoln to a stop out front. Lauren glanced at her wristwatch and saw that it was later than she'd thought.

Not wasting any time, she quickly reached for the coat lying on the seat next to her. It was one thing to sit across from Morgan in a restaurant. It was quite another to be in a dark parked car with him. "It was nice of you to take me to dinner, Morgan. Thank you."

"You're welcome, Lauren," he said, the lines around his mouth tightening as he watched her fumble for the door handle. She was like a frightened little kitten backed into a corner, he thought. He couldn't understand why he should pose such a threat to her. It was true that he'd hurt her, but only because he'd been misguided. He wasn't the man who'd given her a child and left her to fend for herself.

"I hope you enjoyed it," he added.

Lauren was suddenly aware that his voice had taken on a husky tone. She told her mind to ignore the pleasurable sound, but her body quivered in reaction anyway.

"I...I did. And it was...good to see you again, Morgan. Now I think I should say good-night."

Lauren started to open the door, but suddenly Morgan's hand was on her arm. "Lauren, is that all you have to say?"

She looked at him in utter confusion. What was he expecting her to say? she wondered frantically. What could he possibly want to hear?

"I—I don't know what you mean, Morgan. We talked over dinner and—"

Morgan's eyes dropped to where his fingers pressed into her flesh. He hadn't meant for any of this to happen. After four years of her being gone, he'd figured the best thing for him to do was to put her in the past and totally out of his mind. Yet all it had taken was to look at her again to remind him how impossible it would be to ever get her out of his system. "Would you like to get together again?"

Would she? Lauren asked herself. Tonight had been nice, even if it had been difficult at times. But to go out again would probably be asking for trouble. Just a little nudge would have her falling for him all over again. On the other hand, she had to remember that she'd come up here to Mena for the sole purpose of seeing Morgan and telling him about Scott. In order to do that, she'd have to see him again.

"Why?" she asked.

His eyes lifted to her face again. Since the sky was cloudy, the night was very dark, Lauren could just make out the wry twist of his lips. "Does there have to be a reason? I thought you enjoyed tonight."

"I did," she confessed. "But you wouldn't want your girlfriend to get the wrong idea. She might not understand that we're just old friends."

Morgan forced his fingers to loosen their grip on her, but he couldn't bring himself to pull them away. Her skin was like warm velvet, just the way he'd remembered it, and touching her now was every bit as good as it had been then.

"Is that how you think of us, Lauren? As just old friends?"

He could hear the soft intake of her breath. The sound drew his eyes to the thrust of her breasts. Her dress was scooped low at the neckline, and the night shadows played across the gentle swells there.

Suddenly all of the hauntingly familiar things about her blinded him. The compulsion to touch her, to hold her, was too strong to deny.

Lauren felt him inching toward her, but she was too mesmerized to move. This was the man she loved, and even though their lovemaking had caused a traumatic change in her life, it was still one of the sweetest things she'd ever experienced. She'd never been able to forget the feel, the smell, the taste of him.

Before Morgan realized what he was doing, his head lowered and his mouth was pressed to the cleft between her breasts.

Hot and cold sensations rocketed through Lauren at the sudden, unexpected touch. If he had kissed her first she might have been able to resist, but how could she fight the humble urgency of his lips against her breast, so close to her heart?

Her fingers came up and slowly threaded themselves in his curly hair, bringing a groan from Morgan's throat. The erotic sound made Lauren close her eyes against the onslaught of desire coursing through her.

She knew she should push him away, but to do so would be denying her heart everything it had craved throughout the years spent away from him.

Before she could summon up any kind of logic, Morgan raised his head and captured her lips. Suddenly she was pulled into a dark vortex, and all she could do was hang on to him and let his kiss whirl her down into a mindless ecstasy.

The kiss went on and on until the need for breath broke them apart. By then Lauren was dazed and trembling. This was the last thing she had expected to happen, and at the moment she was too stunned to sort anything out.

"Lauren, my God...the things you do to me...even after all this time...."

Lauren swallowed and tried to fight for a measure of sanity. "Morgan...this is...I didn't come up here for this. I came because..."

His hands moved to her face, and he cupped her cheeks in his palms. "Lauren, it doesn't matter why you came. You're here now, and—"

His choice of words brought her crashing back down to earth. Pressing her hands against his chest, she struggled to put some distance between them. But Morgan obviously had other ideas. He wouldn't allow her an inch of breathing space. "Morgan," she said, almost pleading now, "you have no idea how things are with me. And I have no desire to get involved with any man—especially not you."

Morgan's smug chuckle whispered across her cheeks, making her stiffen in her seat. "Is that why you kissed me?"

"I didn't kiss you. You kissed me," she reminded him in a breathy whisper. She wanted to be cross with him, wanted even more to be able to resist him, but at the moment she could manage to do neither.

"A kiss usually takes two."

Lauren sighed helplessly. "Morgan, why are you doing this?"

The despair in her voice tugged at the soft part of him and reminded him that she was no longer the carefree young woman who had once adored him.

His hands dropped from her cheeks and slid into the silky cloud of black hair spilling around her shoulders. "I've missed you, Lauren. Whatever you may think of me, I want you to know that."

Why did everything inside her want to believe the smooth sincerity in his voice? Hadn't all the hurt this man had put her through taught her anything?

"You have a funny way of showing it, Morgan. For four years I heard absolutely nothing from you. That tells me exactly how much you've missed me. Now please let me go in," she said, her voice growing sharp with remembered pain.

He eased away from her but still did not let her go completely. "I want to see you again, Lauren. Things were never finished between us. Not in my book."

Lauren's brows lifted. "I think you need to remember that I'm twenty-two, Morgan, not nineteen. I don't believe everything that comes out of your mouth now."

Morgan's sigh was filled with frustration. "Lauren, I'm not your enemy. I want the chance to prove that to you."

He might not be her enemy, Lauren thought, but he had the power to hurt her all over again. The kiss they'd just shared proved that all too vividly. But then there was Scott, she thought desperately. He was her sole purpose in life, the sole reason she was with Morgan now. She had to remember that.

"I don't want to fight with you, Morgan."

"Good," he said with sudden cheerfulness. "So how would you and Scott like to go on a picnic?"

Lauren couldn't have been more stunned. "A picnic!"

She repeated the word as though it were foreign, Morgan thought. And maybe it was to her. Lauren had told him she worked six days a week. That would hardly leave time for her to enjoy a leisurely outing like a picnic.

"Yes. I thought your son might enjoy being in the woods. Especially if he's like his mother."

Your son. The words brought a guilty pang to Lauren's heart. She looked up into Morgan's face. At present his strong features were hidden by shadows—just as his motives and feelings were hidden, she supposed.

What would he think, how would he react, if he knew Scott was his son, too? The thought made her tremble. "Scott loves the outdoors," she said with thoughtful reserve. "And it would give him a chance to get acquainted with the woods. This is all quite a change for him. Mena's nothing like downtown Houston."

Smiling with satisfaction, Morgan leaned back in his seat. "You should show him all you can before you go back," he told her. "I'll pick you up about ten, Saturday morning."

There was no use protesting, she thought. And why should she? This was what she wanted, wasn't it? "If you really insist," she said.

"I'm not insisting, Lauren. I'm asking."

"Oh, all right, then. We'll be ready." Clutching her coat protectively against her, Lauren opened the door before he had a chance to go around and do it for her. "Good night, Morgan."

"Good night."

The house was quiet as Lauren got out the key to let herself in. As she did, Morgan's Lincoln pulled away from the drive. For a moment she watched the taillights disappear into the darkness. The sight left her feeling forlorn, and she hurried to unlock the door.

As she stepped into the house, Lauren realized that the whole evening had left her filled with regret and hope. Being with Morgan reminded her that she still loved him as much as ever, which was something she regretted if she ever expected to get on with her life. Yet, on the other hand, she had some reason to be a bit hopeful. He'd been warm with her and that was something she'd never expected. At times she could almost have let herself believe he still cared for her. Which was foolish, because she knew he didn't. Still, just the fact that he hadn't turned her away led her to hope that he might eventually come to care about Scott.

Her mother and Scott were obviously asleep, though a fire was still burning in the fireplace. After putting her mother's coat away in the closet, she crossed the living room to the armchair that sat on one side of the hearth.

Lauren sat there for a long time, staring into the flames, remembering the past and wondering what the future was going to hold for all three of them.

She supposed a lot of that depended on her. After all, she held the key. Perhaps she should go on back to Houston and put the whole idea out of her mind. Aunt Hattie had said she would eventually find a man who would love her and treat Scott as his own. Maybe that was possible. But how could she have any kind of marriage if she still loved Morgan? And how could she let Scott think some other man was his father?

That would be living a lie, and she didn't think she could ever be happy living under such circumstances.

Several minutes passed more before Lauren finally roused herself and went to get ready for bed. The bedroom was chilly, and she undressed hurriedly. But once she climbed into bed, the patchwork country quilts quickly warmed her.

Scott was curled in a ball beside her, his breathing deep with sleep. She brushed a kiss against his baby-soft cheek, then snuggled her head down into the pillow beside him and willed her mind to sleep.

An hour later she was still wide-awake, and angry with herself because she couldn't get the sudden, impulsive embrace she and Morgan had shared out of her mind.

She was certain that it hadn't meant anything on his part. He'd probably only done it out of curiosity, to see if she would respond.

Well, she thought, disgusted with herself, she sure hadn't disappointed him in that department. The memory of his kiss still filled her with heat, and she knew with a kind of dread that if he should want her to repeat the performance she'd respond to him all over again. It was a painful thought.

The next day held beautiful weather. At times November in Arkansas could be as warm as summer, and Lauren almost felt as if she were back in Texas as the warm sun beat down on her and Scott.

The two of them were walking hand in hand along the wide sidewalk. Downtown Mena was not all that big, and Lauren had already shown Scott most of it. She knew he wasn't really old enough to appreciate the difference between these small-town streets and the busier ones in Houston. To him it was all just buildings and cars. But she knew Scott enjoyed being outdoors and, in particular, having this time alone with his mother.

At the next corner Lauren guided Scott down the street to their left. "This is the way to my friend's place," she told him. "Want to go see her?"

"Is she nice, Mama?"

Lauren chuckled to herself. "Of course she's nice, Scott. And I'll bet she's going to be really tickled to see you."

"Is she old?"

"She's like me," Lauren told him with an amused smile.

"Does she have candy?"

Lauren looked down at her young son. "Scott!" she said softly. "Do you think you should get candy everywhere you go?"

"Yes!" he cried, giggling uproariously when she made a face at him.

A bell tinkled over the glass door as Lauren and Scott entered Gypsy's salon. The air reeked with ammonia, cigarette smoke and hair spray. Several women sat under hooded driers, and two more were being worked over in styling chairs.

Gypsy was at one of the chairs, her multiringed hands waving in the air as she related a story to the woman sitting in front of her.

"I think you have another customer, Gypsy," the woman told her when she spotted Lauren and Scott in the mirror.

Gypsy turned to look, and Lauren laughed when her friend's mouth dropped open.

"Lauren!" she squealed, so loudly that even the women under the driers lifted their heads to look. "Lauren! My Lord, I can't believe it's you!"

The tall, long-legged brunette rushed toward the two of them and crushed Lauren in a welcoming embrace.

She began firing questions at Lauren. "What are you doing here? When did you get home?"

Lauren laughed at her friend's excitement. "I got here Sunday," she told her.

Her face beaming, Gypsy looked down at the small boy clinging to his mother's hand.

"And this is Scott, I'll bet. Right?" she asked him.

He nodded, and Gypsy squatted down to his level. "Oh, boy, are you ever going to make hearts pitter-pat," she said with a wide grin for him. "You look like your Mama, did you know that, Scott?"

The child nodded again, making both Lauren and Gypsy laugh.

"Are you having fun with your grandma?" Gypsy asked him.

"She lets me feed the dog, and he's big and hairy," Scott told her.

Gypsy nodded and glanced up at Lauren with a wry grin. "He's yours, all right."

"You're pretty. Like Mama," he said to Gypsy.

Her wide mouth parted in surprise, and then she laughed. "Why, you little darlin'! Aren't you sweet!" She hugged him, then hauled him onto her hip. "I'm not really pretty like your mama. Mine's all paint, Scott. But you'll learn that when you get older."

"Gypsy! For Pete's sake." Lauren laughed.

Gypsy chuckled saucily and started back to her customer, who was still waiting patiently, and motioned for Lauren to follow her.

For the next few minutes Gypsy introduced the two of them to all the customers and to her co-worker. Lauren didn't know any of them, and she was secretly relieved. It would be difficult to deal with any pointed questions about her sudden departure from Mena four years ago. Other than her mother and Gypsy, no one knew why Lauren had really left her home...or why she'd stayed in Houston.

By the time Lauren and Scott left the salon, Gypsy had agreed to join them for supper that evening. Lauren drove home with lifted spirits. Gypsy had a way of doing that. Seeing her old friend again was just the balm Lauren had needed. They had always kept up with each other through letters, but being able to talk to Gypsy at her leisure was something Lauren was looking forward to.

"I'm so glad Gypsy could come out tonight," Eileen said later that evening as she and Lauren prepared supper. "But I wish I'd have known sooner. I would have gotten something special at the market."

Lauren laughed as she diligently browned onions

and garlic in a black iron skillet. "Gypsy eats any-thing. Surely you haven't forgotten that."

"No, I haven't forgotten. But pork chops could hardly be described as special," Eileen replied as she dropped the floured meat into another skillet. "Was Gypsy surprised to see you?"

"She squealed so loud the windows rattled." Lau-ren laughed. "It was so good to see her, Mom. I guess I just never stopped to think how much I've missed home and my friends."

Eileen reached for a long fork and arranged the chops in the hot skillet. "You've been too busy taking care of Scott and yourself," she said. "But I'm so glad you had this chance to come back home." She gave her daughter a sidelong glance. "I guess...well, I guess I've been hoping you wouldn't want to go back to Houston once you got here among all your friends again."

Lauren was surprised by her mother's admission. She'd never realized Eileen wanted her here that much.

"Mom..." she began guardedly. "It wouldn't be wise for me to stay in Mena. I thought you knew that's how I felt."

Eileen shrugged. "I do know that's how you feel. But if you're going to tell Morgan about Scott, what reason would you have for not wanting to stay?"

Lauren poured a can of tomatoes over the onions and garlic, then glanced over at the kitchen table, where Scott sat quietly, playing with a piece of pie dough his grandma had given him. "My job, for one."

"You could work in a salon here."

Lauren grimaced as she continued to stir in a cup of dried rice. "Yes. At a cut in pay." She looked over at her mother. "Gypsy has to give two perms to almost make what I do on just one. I think she's crazy for doing it."

Eileen's expression remained as serene as ever. "This isn't Houston, darling. The cost of living is different. And Gypsy lives here because this is where her family and friends are."

Lauren covered the Spanish rice with a heavy lid. "So you're saying I should be like Gypsy."

Eileen sighed. "I'm saying that money isn't everything."

Reaching up, Lauren pushed at the wayward curls on her forehead. "I find it hard to agree with that, Mom. I think money had a lot to do with Morgan pushing me out of his life."

"Lauren!"

"It's true and you know it," she said bitterly. "He kept saying I was too young to be his wife. But I think it was more like too poor to be his wife."

As Eileen opened her mouth to protest, a knock sounded on the door. Relieved to end the conversation, Lauren went to answer it and found Gypsy on the other side.

The brunette was vivacious and candid and had Scott giggling before two minutes had passed. She helped Lauren and Eileen finish the meal while telling them all the latest things going on in her life.

It wasn't until the meal was over and the dishes were cleaned and put away that Eileen said she intended to take Scott over to some friends for a little visit.

Lauren figured her mother was doing it to give her and Gypsy some time to be alone together. Eileen probably figured giving Lauren extra time with her old friend would help persuade her to stay in Mena. Subtle conniving, Lauren thought wryly. But she'd already learned that it was a mother's prerogative to be that way sometimes.

"Gosh, I forget how long it's been since I came out here," Gypsy said as she and Lauren settled down in front of the fireplace with a cup of after-dinner coffee. "I see your mother in town sometimes. And she comes in and gets a perm now and then. I just never seem to have the time to drive out here and see her."

Lauren leaned back in her armchair. "I suppose the last time you were here was the night I packed to leave for Houston."

Gypsy frowned. "I was very mad at you then."

"I remember," Lauren replied dryly. "I was looking to you for comfort and support, and all you could do was tell me how stupid I was acting."

"That's because you were," Gypsy told her, pulling out a cigarette and lighting it with a dramatic flourish.

A fond smile curved Lauren's lips as she watched

her friend. Gypsy had always done everything with a flourish. The two of them were very different people, but for some reason they went together like paper and glue.

"Tell me," Gypsy went on, "have you seen Morgan yet?"

Lauren almost choked on her coffee. "You never did have much tact, Gypsy. I can see you haven't changed a bit."

"Bull," Gypsy said, waving her cigarette in the air. "What is tact between friends?"

Lauren looked away from her friend and over at the crackling fire. "I guess you're right."

"I was always right where you were concerned," Gypsy said with exaggerated conceit. "So tell me, have you seen him?"

Lauren nodded. "Yes. As a matter of fact, we had dinner together last night."

"Thank God!"

Lauren's eyes swung around to her friend. "What is that supposed to mean?"

"Just what it says. Back here with Morgan is where you've always belonged."

Lauren snorted. "Well, don't draw any big conclusions just because we had dinner."

Gypsy actually laughed. "I'm drawing big conclusions because you were within grabbing distance of each other. That's all you and Morgan need. Just take my word for it."

If grabbing were all there was to it, things would already be settled, Lauren thought dismally. They'd certainly grabbed for a few seconds last night. But that was the last thing Gypsy needed to know.

"Gypsy, all those ammonia and peroxide fumes are getting to you," Lauren said. "You know better than anyone that Morgan will never think of me as someone he'd want in his life permanently."

Gypsy frowned and stubbed out her cigarette. "And how many times have I asked you why?"

"A thousand, probably, and each time I've answered you the same way. I'm from poor hillbilly stock. That's not a Sinclair's style."

"Damn that poor-little-Lauren stuff," Gypsy retorted. "You're a beautiful, intelligent young woman. You could spin Morgan around on his heels if you tried."

"I don't think I could even if I wanted to," Lauren said. "He's heartless."

"You didn't use to think so. You have Scott to prove that."

Her cheeks flaming, Lauren put her coffee aside and walked over to the hearth. "I discovered Morgan's true feathers later," she said finally.

"If he's so heartless, why did you go out with him last night?"

For a moment Lauren closed her eyes, trying to ward off the image of Morgan's face drawing nearer and nearer, the memory of his lips tasting hers.

"To decide if I should tell him about Scott," Lauren answered.

"And what did you decide?" Gypsy wanted to know.

"I haven't yet."

"You haven't!"

"Gypsy, please, I invited you over here to talk about old times, not about Morgan!"

"Face it, Lauren. Your old times *are* Morgan. When we were together that was all I ever heard out of you—Morgan this and Morgan that. You were crazy about the guy. And I can't say I blame you. The man is gorgeous, and rich to boot." *Gorgeous and rich.* It was strange that Lauren never thought of him in those terms. To her he was a part of her heart that had been torn away and never replaced. He was the man she loved, pure and simple.

Lauren looked anxiously over at her old friend. "Gypsy," she said in a low voice, "how do you think he'll react to hearing that Scott is his?"

Gypsy pursed her lips, then pushed herself out of her chair. "I think he'll be outraged," she said, joining Lauren by the hearth. "But once he gets over it, he's going to be crazy about both of you."

Lauren groaned. "Oh, my dear friend, you have such a wonderful way of putting things."

Gypsy grinned and flung her long, dark hair over one shoulder. "Mama always thought so, too."

Lauren chuckled in spite of everything. "So tell me, smarty, why haven't you gotten married?"

"I'm too young to get married. And besides that, I know all the bachelors around here too well. Familiarity takes away the spark, you know."

Lauren's brows lifted with amusement. "Maybe someone new will move into town," she suggested.

"I've decided if that doesn't happen in the next six months I'm going to write to a lonely-hearts club."

That drew fits of laughter from both women, and for a while Lauren was able to put Morgan out of her mind.

Gypsy stayed until late that night. Lauren said good-night to her old friend and went to bed with a better perspective on things. She only hoped she could hold on to the optimism until Saturday, when Morgan came to pick her and Scott up for the picnic.

Chapter Six

By ten o'clock Saturday morning, Lauren and Scott were dressed and waiting for Morgan.

The sky was beautifully clear and promised to hold warm Indian-summer weather. Lauren had dressed Scott in brown cords and a long-sleeved T-shirt in bright yellow. For herself she'd chosen a well-worn pair of blue jeans and a moss-green sweater, and had tied her black hair back with a matching ribbon.

Lauren hadn't heard from Morgan since the night they'd had dinner. She didn't know whether to be relieved about that or not. It could be that he was having second thoughts about spending time with her and Scott. But then, she supposed, if he felt that way he would have called with some excuse and canceled the outing.

In truth, everything about Morgan's behavior puzzled Lauren, and for the past few days she'd thought of little else. The things he'd said to her, the way he'd looked at her and the way he'd touched her had all filled her with deeply mixed emotions. Maybe today would shed some light on his intentions. She certainly hoped so, because time was slipping by quickly. If she was going to go through with her initial plan, she was going to have to do it soon.

Scott began to bounce on his toes and squeal, bringing Lauren out of her deep reverie.

"He's here, Mama! He's here!"

Lauren looked out the picture window. Morgan was walking through the front gate.

"I gotta have my sweatshirt on," Scott cried in excitement. He still couldn't quite manage some of his clothing. In his eagerness to be ready, he thrust his right arm in the wrong sleeve, then frowned with frustration when he couldn't figure out where the left one was.

"Just calm down," Lauren told him with patient indulgence. "Let me help you."

Morgan knocked on the door before she finished zipping up Scott's sweatshirt and tying the hood over his head.

"Come in," she called, without bothering to look up. She didn't have to look to know the moment Morgan stepped through the door.

"Hello, Lauren."

At the sound of his voice she turned toward him, and her heart missed a beat. He was smiling at her. Smiling as though he really wanted to be with her. It was impossible to remain cool and indifferent under Morgan's particular brand of warmth.

"Hello, Morgan," she said, wondering why her voice, which had been perfectly normal a moment ago, now sounded tremulous.

"Are you ready for a picnic?" he said, addressing the young boy.

Scott nodded, though with less exuberance than he had shown earlier.

"Scott's been excited about this picnic ever since I told him about it. But you're a stranger, and he's not quite sure about you yet," Lauren said, explaining the child's shyness.

Morgan grinned and knelt down next to Scott. "Can you tell me your name, little guy?"

Scott's green eyes grew large as he carefully appraised Morgan. Then, seemingly satisfied that this big man was going to be a friend, he blurted out with a toothy grin, "Scott Magee."

Morgan winced at the Magee part but made himself push it aside. "Well, my name is Morgan. Can you say that?"

Scott nodded slowly, then carefully mouthed the unfamiliar name. "Morgan."

Morgan chuckled, then reached for the boy's hand. "Tell me, Scott, do you like fried chicken?"

"Yeah!"

Lauren broke in. "Morgan! Did you bring food?"

He looked at her. "Yes. It was my invitation, remember?"

"But I fixed a whole basket of food, too," she told him.

Morgan looked back at the cute little face that was still staring intently up at him. "Then me and you are going to have to do a whole lot of eatin', aren't we, Scott?"

Scott nodded and giggled. With a sudden turn, he trotted toward the kitchen. "Show him, Mama. Come show him."

Lauren had left the wicker hamper she'd packed earlier sitting on the kitchen table. With a wry smile, Morgan lifted the lid to see that it was filled with sandwiches and all sorts of side dishes.

"You shouldn't have gone to all this trouble, Lauren. But look at it this way—now we can stay and eat supper, too," he said, turning a charming smile on her. "If you want to get a jacket, I'll take Scott and the basket on out to the truck."

Unable to help herself, she smiled back at him and nodded. "I'll just be a minute," she told him, watching with a sort of sweet pain as Scott left the room clinging to his father's hand.

Morgan was driving a shiny red Ford Ranger today. By the time he'd loaded the food basket in the back and settled Scott in the front seat Lauren had arrived with a jacket stuffed under her arm.

Scott had seldom ridden in a pickup truck, and as Morgan drove them down the graveled road the child looked around in silent awe.

"It's very generous of you to spend your Saturday with us," Lauren said.

"I have a foreman at the mill who keeps things running smoothly without me," he told her. "I can usually take off whenever I want."

"I can't imagine what that must feel like," she admitted. "This is the first vacation I've had in four years."

That meant ever since she'd been in Houston, he calculated. He'd often wondered why she'd never come home, even for just a short visit. He'd even asked Eileen about it, but Lauren's mother had managed to evade the question by saying it was too hard for Lauren to get away from her job. Maybe he'd been conceited to think she'd stayed in Houston all this time to avoid him.

"It sounds like you work too hard," he said casually, hoping she'd relax and open up to him.

"I'm young," she said with a shrug of her slender shoulders. "Now is the time for me to work hard and save money."

His brown eyes slanted away from the road to glance at her. As Lauren met his gaze, she had to admit that he looked very sexy this morning. His broad shoulders were covered with a neutral-colored sweater of cable knit. A pair of Levi's were molded to his thick, muscular thighs, and white jogging shoes replaced the cowboy boots he wore to work.

Morgan had always been most comfortable when he was outdoors. She supposed his love of nature and open spaces was one of the things that had drawn her to him.

"You've mentioned making money several times

since you've been back home. That surprises me,
Lauren. Money matters never worried you before."

A dry retort rose to her lips, but Lauren bit it back.
He hadn't meant to be unkind. Actually, there had
been a hint of concern in his voice. She told herself
to warm to his sincerity and not dwell on the hurt
he'd caused her in the past.

"Before I didn't have a son to worry about. I want
to make sure his future is secure."

Frowning, Morgan said, "Somehow I think it's
more than that."

By now they were on the main highway, headed
into town. Lauren kept her eyes on the mountains
outside the windows. "Why do you say that? You act
as if it's strange that I take Scott's welfare so seriously."

"You're young, Lauren. My Lord, you need time
off from the pressures of work, even if you think you
can't afford it."

She sighed. He couldn't understand how it was for
her. He might not understand even if he knew Scott
was his.

"I'm not young anymore, Morgan. I may look it
on the outside, but on the inside I'm old as dirt."

He couldn't believe her cynicism. He didn't want
to believe she even harbored such feelings. Four years
ago she'd been young and fresh and filled with an
unusual zest for life. He wanted that Lauren back.
Each moment he spent with her he yearned for her
more and more.

"Dirt," Scott repeated, picking up his mother's

word. It was one he was very familiar with. "There's dirt, Mama."

Morgan chuckled as Scott pointed to the bare earth alongside the highway. "Your Mama's not as old as dirt, is she Scott?"

Scott shook his black head with comical vigor, and suddenly a laugh burst from Lauren.

The deep, husky sound of her pleasure brought Morgan's eyes back to her. It was infinitely sweet to hear her laugh, and he was suddenly filled with joy at the fact that she'd finally come home—with or without a child.

Once they reached town, Morgan turned east and headed up into the mountains on Highway 1. It was basically a scenic route running through a portion of the Ouachita National Forest. On the uppermost ridge of Rich Mountain was the Queen Wilhelmina State Park with its lodge. Lauren supposed that Morgan had decided to have the picnic there.

In spite of its being late autumn, they found many cars and visitors at the lodge. The gray rock structure was stately in size and design, a big attraction for tourists from both Arkansas and Oklahoma. For most of the year it was overrun with guests.

The green lawns sloped gently away from the lodge for several hundred yards before reaching the picnic area, with its small zoo and railroad track. When Morgan failed to stop at either one, Lauren looked at him curiously.

"Where are we going, anyway?" she asked.

"Farther into the mountains, away from all these

tourists. I want Scott to see the woods, not a bunch of people clicking their cameras. We can always stop on the way back if he'd like to see the zoo and the train.''

Lauren wasn't about to argue with that. In fact, she was inwardly pleased that they would be able to enjoy their lunch in privacy.

''That sounds fine,'' she agreed.

Morgan drove the three of them fifteen miles farther along the mountain ridges. At various places the obscuring trees gave way to spectacular views of the valley floor far below them. Scott was enthralled by it all. His pointing and his excited chatter continued until Morgan turned onto a dirt road leading into the woods.

Lauren didn't know how she could have forgotten about this particular secluded camping area. She and Morgan had picnicked up here a long time ago. They'd gotten caught in a thunderstorm and been soaked to the skin. But the wet clothes hadn't stopped them from having fun. Once the rain had ended, they'd spent the whole day exploring the woods and simply being together.

But that had been when they were in love—or at least *she* had been, Lauren thought.

The pickup wobbled over the rough road. While Lauren steadied Scott on the seat, she hazarded a glance at Morgan. Had he intentionally brought her here to this place? she wondered.

No, why should he? she answered herself crossly. Why should he want to remind her of those times?

Besides, he could have had any number of girls up here since then. It probably meant nothing to him now.

Morgan felt her eyes upon him and turned to look at her. "Do you remember this place, Lauren?"

She nodded, wondering if he could read her mind. "Yes. Our clothes were so wet that after the sun did eventually come out we literally steamed for about two hours."

He grinned faintly as he pulled the truck into a graveled parking area. "Your mother had sent along some of her cinnamon rolls just for me. I think I ate more than a dozen of them before the day was out."

"You ate like a hog back then, Morgan," Lauren told him teasingly. "I always thought it was unfair that you never got fat."

He laughed as he shut off the engine, then turned and gave Scott a tickle on the tummy. "We're gonna show your mama that hogs don't have anything on us today. Right, Scott?"

"Yep! Hogs!" Scott repeated joyfully, making Lauren groan in response.

"Morgan, I'm trying to teach him good manners," she said, "and here you are talking about hogs. You'll probably be showing him how to spit watermelon seeds, too, I guess."

Morgan smiled devilishly and winked at Scott. "Did you bring watermelon?"

Scott nodded and Lauren said, "Mother had a few down in the cellar. They're the small late ones she grew in the garden. I thought I'd bring one."

"Good. We'll have a contest with the seeds. I bet Scott can spit one farther than anybody."

"Oh, no, Morgan Sinclair," Lauren retorted while Scott giggled about the whole thing. "If I see you showing him how to spit even one seed I'll throw every one of these blasted cinnamon rolls in the creek."

Lauren opened the door and began to climb out of the truck. Morgan looked at her with a surprised but hopeful expression. "Your mother sent cinnamon rolls? For me?"

"She did," Lauren informed him, reaching into the back for the wicker hamper. "For some reason, she's always been partial to you, Morgan."

"Hmmm," he purred like a proud tomcat. "Probably because I'm good-looking, charming, and have a terribly sweet personality—as long as I have my own way about things."

Morgan reached into the truck and lifted Scott out and down to the ground.

Lauren watched him retie the string of Scott's hood with a gentleness that made her heart weep. Her mother had said Morgan was a good man. Could Lauren have misjudged him so severely? If he was so good, why had he sent her away?

She swallowed down the thickness in her throat, thinking that she wanted to enjoy today, not dwell on past hurt and anger. Forcing a smile, she said, "I'm sure that's exactly what endears you to her. Especially that last part, Morgan."

He stood up from tying Scott's sweatshirt and cast

her an enigmatic look. "I used to endear myself to her daughter," he stated with sudden seriousness.

Lauren felt hot color rush to her cheeks. "Yes, you endeared yourself to me," she said, knowing that not to agree would have made her a liar. "But I was young and impressionable then. That was when I still had a hillbilly heart. I don't anymore."

He didn't say anything, but walked around the pickup to where she stood. Bored with the adults' conversation, Scott wandered over to one of the cement picnic tables and began exploring it.

"I liked your hillbilly heart, Lauren. Why didn't you want to keep it?"

Lauren found she couldn't look at him. It was too painful.

"Because that heart was ignorant and trusting. It thought all hearts were created equal." Somehow she managed to lift her green eyes up to his. "But you forced it to face facts, Morgan. I guess I should thank you for that."

Morgan frowned, not liking the pain shadowed in her eyes. "Apparently I didn't change it as much as you thought," he said appraisingly. "You must have trusted Scott's father—for a time."

Her face suddenly blanched, and she blindly hefted the picnic basket over the side of pickup. "I don't want to talk about Scott's father," she said hoarsely.

Morgan quickly reached out and touched her arm. "I'm sorry, Lauren. Forget I said that. I want us to have a fun day today. Just like we used to, okay?"

When she didn't respond immediately, he chucked her gently under the chin. "Okay, honey?"

Lauren took a deep breath and nodded. She wanted the same thing. She also knew she couldn't keep letting each little thing he said tear her apart.

Smiling faintly, she said, "I want the same thing. So do you think we could eat on the ground instead of using a table?"

Grinning, he reached into the pickup bed and brought out a folded piece of oilcloth. "I'm way ahead of you, Lauren. Let's pick out a spot," he suggested.

Instead of using the camping areas, where many of the trees had been cleared away, she and Morgan chose to have their picnic near a small stream several yards down the slope of the mountain. The trees made a thick canopy over their heads, and the smell of pine was sharp and tangy in the air.

Fall rains had made the ground damp and musky-smelling, but there was a heavy carpet of leaves where they could spread the oilcloth.

While Lauren put out the food, Morgan took Scott down near the stream to allow the child a closer look. There was not another soul around for miles, and the silence was wonderful.

The birdcalls and the gentle rush of the breeze in the pines were so tranquil compared to a busy salon where the telephone rang constantly throughout the day. Not to mention several blow-driers buzzing while women gossiped. Lauren supposed she'd grown accustomed to it all. But, oh, how she'd missed this forest and home.

Since there were two baskets of food, Lauren chose food from each one so that there would be a wide selection. As she finished her task, she shifted her position so that she could watch Morgan and Scott.

Morgan was showing the boy how to skip a flat pebble across the water. Of course, Scott was too small to have much arm and hand control, but he was having great fun throwing the rocks anyway. His giggles and his animated voice carried through the quiet woods, punctuated by Morgan's deeper tone.

The sight of them together was poignant for Lauren. She kept thinking that this was how it should have been in the past. The way it should be in the future.

But all things were not possible, she reasoned. Morgan had not wanted to marry her, and without the family structure that marriage brought, he could hardly be a full-time father to Scott.

Lauren had come to terms with that fact a long time ago. Now she could only hope that he would accept Scott as his child and perhaps be willing to spend a few days with him during the year. It was not all she dreamed of for Scott, but it would be better than no father at all.

"I've got everything ready if you guys are hungry," Lauren told the two of them.

Morgan glanced over his shoulder to see that Lauren had joined them. He thought again how beautiful she looked. Somehow the sylvan surroundings added

to her earthy beauty, and he wished with a bit of guilt
that the two of them were alone. He wanted to make
love to her, to worship her with his heart and his
body. He wanted to show her that all the fire, love
and need he felt for her were still there inside him.

"I'm ready," Morgan answered. Then he looked
down at his newfound friend. "How 'bout you,
Scott?"

Scott shook his head. "I wanna throw rocks."

"Scott..." Lauren began.

"We'll come back and throw rocks after we eat,"
Morgan said cajolingly. "We might even find a crawdad."

"Crawdad?" Scott repeated curiously. "What's a
crawdad?"

Morgan looked up at Lauren with a twisted grin.
"What have you been teaching this child, Lauren?"

She chuckled. "It's rather hard to find crawdads in
downtown Houston, unless we order some boiled Ca-
jun ones to eat."

Laughing, Morgan reached down and hefted Scott
in one arm. The three of them started back up the
steep incline.

"A crawdad," he told Scott, who was listening in
great earnest, "is an ugly little creature that swims
backwards and has whiskers and fingers to pinch
you." As if to stress his last words, he gave Scott a
gentle little pinch on the belly that produced a toothy
grin from the child.

Smiling, Lauren told Scott, "Morgan's kinda like
a crawdad. He pinches and he has whiskers. See?"

She put her hand up to Morgan's jaw and let her fingers slide over the faint edging of beard he'd neglected to shave off this morning. "In fact, he can even swim backward when he tries hard enough."

Lauren's casual touch seared Morgan with longing, and he wondered if everything he felt showed in his eyes. Maybe it did, because she was suddenly looking away from him as if she regretted having touched him. The idea hurt Morgan. She'd once loved to touch him.

The meal was pleasant for all three of them. As expected, Morgan stuffed himself on the cinnamon rolls and Lauren made a pig of herself with the fried chicken Morgan had packed in his cache.

By the time they'd finished eating and Lauren had stored away the food, the two adults were full and lazy. Scott, however, was still eager to explore all the new sights and sounds around him.

For the next hour he showed little sign of slowing down, but then Morgan happened to spot a red squirrel up in a hickory tree. The child was fascinated and sat quietly watching the animal's comings and goings as he gathered nuts and stored them in a hole in the tree trunk.

Tears welled up in Scott's eyes when the animal finally scampered away. "I want the squirrel to come back, Mama."

"He's gone to be with the other squirrels," Lauren explained. "He'll come back for his nuts when he gets hungry."

"Hmm, hungry. That reminds me.... It's about time to eat again, isn't it?" Morgan said to Lauren.

"Eat again! Morgan, you're a bottomless pit!"

He gave her a crooked grin. "Well, we could have some coffee and another cinnamon roll."

She rolled her eyes in disbelief at his appetite. "There are only two left."

"Just right. One for me and one for you." He winked at her, then reached for Scott's hand. "Come on, boy, I know just the thing for you."

While Lauren got the coffee and rolls, Morgan hacked a small limb off a hickory tree and brought it and Scott back to their makeshift pallet on the ground.

The child watched with dark, curious eyes as Morgan used his pocketknife to cut off a four-inch piece of the limb and began to whittle it carefully into a shape. After a few minutes Morgan handed it to him.

"Now put this end in your mouth and blow," Morgan instructed the boy.

The whistle gave a sharp shrill, and Scott's eyes widened in astonishment. "A whistle!" he chortled gleefully. "Mama, a whistle!"

Lauren smiled and ruffled his hair. The weather had long ago grown warm enough for them to remove Scott's hood, and now his black curls glistened in the sunlight.

"Morgan's pretty clever, isn't he?" she asked her son. Scott nodded.

Then, in a gesture that surprised both adults, the child hugged Morgan's neck and plastered a wet kiss on his cheek. "Thank you, Morgan."

"You're welcome, partner," Morgan said huskily, returning the child's hug.

Thrilled with his new toy, Scott wandered near the adults and sounded off on the whistle. Morgan stretched out on the oilcloth and savored the last bite of cinnamon roll. Lauren was content to sit cross-legged and sip her coffee from a Styrofoam cup.

"You must know how much your patience with Scott means to me," she told him. "This day is something he'll talk about for a long time to come."

"Don't thank me, Lauren. I've probably enjoyed Scott more than he has me."

"I doubt it," Lauren said, wrinkling her nose at him. "I think you've just become his hero."

Morgan brushed a few crumbs from his midsection and cut his brown eyes over at her. "Does he— He hasn't been around many men, has he?"

Lauren shook her head. "I know it's not a good thing. He is around my uncle, but since Bob holds down two jobs, he rarely has any time to spend with Scott. I wish my father was alive," she said wistfully. "At least then Scott would have a grandfather."

Morgan wanted to ask her if Scott had a grandfather on the paternal side, but he stopped himself. She'd said she didn't want to talk about Scott's father. Obviously it was still painful for her, and that could only mean she still felt something for the man. Morgan discovered he despised the idea.

"Well, I wouldn't worry about it. It won't be long until he starts school, and then he'll be around plenty of boys. So I wouldn't be thinking about finding a

man just—well, just for Scott." Now why the hell
had he felt the need to say that? She'd probably tell
him to stick his nose back in his own business.

Lauren's eyes swiftly darted away from his. "I'm
not," she told him, trying to keep her voice casual.

Morgan was immensely relieved, though he knew
it was crazy. It was obvious she had no intention of
becoming involved with him again, or of staying permanently in Mena. She'd put him out of her life completely. That was what he should have done, he supposed. But Morgan had learned quickly that love
could not be dictated to.

She looked back at him and felt her heart go thud-
thud. "Would you like to have children, Morgan?"

His brows inched lazily upward. "Of course I'd
like to have children. I thought you knew all those
years ago that I wanted children."

She swallowed to ease the sudden dryness in her
throat. "That was a long time ago, and people can
change their minds. And since you don't have children, I thought...well, that maybe..."

His chuckle held a note of disbelief. "Lauren, I'm
not even married," he told her.

Her eyes grew somber. "Neither am I."

Chapter Seven

Sighing regretfully, Morgan raked his fingers through his hair. Some few yards away, Scott blew his wooden whistle.

"Damn, I'm sorry, Lauren. I didn't think—"

"Forget it," she said tightly.

Lauren was sitting fairly close to him, and it was no effort for Morgan to reach out and close his fingers around her wrist. His touch was both pain and magic, and she wondered if he felt the rapid tripping of her pulse.

"No," he insisted. "I don't want you to think I was trying to put you down. You said I'd acted like a judgmental ass that first day I saw you. And maybe I did. But I was shocked to see you with a child."

Lauren set her coffee cup against the tree trunk behind her and looked over at Scott to make sure he wasn't getting into anything harmful.

"I don't know why, Morgan," she told him. "I've been gone a long time. A lot could have happened in my life without you knowing about it."

She forced herself to swing her gaze back to him. Her heart lurched when she met his eyes. It was impossible to deny the pain in his face. Her skin burned where he was touching her, and she felt as if her senses were splintering in all directions. What did it mean?

"Lauren, I always thought it would be you and me. I'd always planned on that."

Pain practically paralyzed her throat. "Morgan, how can you say that? You told me to go away—anywhere, as long as it was away from you."

With a groan of frustration, Morgan reached up and rubbed his face with both hands.

"I told you much more than that, Lauren, but you were either too young or too obstinate to listen."

She gasped. "Morgan! I was in love with you! It wasn't hero worship, and it wasn't teenage infatuation. I loved you with all my heart. How could you expect me to hear anything except—except get out of my life?"

She'd loved him! She *had* loved him! It was amazing to Morgan just how much her use of the past tense hurt. It also amazed him to know how much he yearned to hear her say she loved him now. Were all men as foolish as he?

"Lauren," he began, "I was five years older than you—"

"You still are," she quickly interjected. "That was and is something that will never change."

He muttered something unintelligible, then turned his vivid brown eyes directly on her. "Yes, it does change. When both people are older and more mature."

Her black lashes fell to partially hide her eyes. "You're saying I wasn't mature enough to love you?"

"Don't twist my words, Lauren," he pleaded.

She took a deep breath and told herself not to lose control. "I just— It's hard for me to understand you, Morgan. You said you loved me, but you sent me away. Now you say I've hurt you and that you'd always planned on us being together." She shook her head. "None of that makes sense to me."

Suddenly he shifted to a sitting position and carefully clasped both her hands in his. "That's because you made everything black-and-white, Lauren. For you it was just stay or go. You and me, together or apart."

She felt her eyes melting into the warmth of his brown ones. "That's the way it must be for lovers," she said with quiet conviction.

Morgan ached with a raw need, the need to love her and have her love him in return.

"Back then you were too young to be my lover, or my wife. But that didn't mean I wanted you out of my life completely."

Could she really believe that? "Then why did you push me out of your life?"

He grimaced, as though her question was as painful to him as it was to her. "Because there didn't seem to be any other way. I tried to tell you how I felt, but you kept seeing it as rejection."

She swallowed. "It was."

He shook his head and gripped her hands a bit tighter. "I wanted you to have the chance to enjoy the last of your young years, to go to college if you wanted, be carefree and experience all the things you'd never get to experience if you were tied down to a husband and children. I'd had my chance at all of that, and I wanted you to have the same."

"Am I supposed to look at that as a magnanimous gesture on your part?" she asked dryly.

"No. Because I would have felt guilty as hell if I didn't give you that chance. I also worried that if we married you would eventually realize all that I'd taken away from you, that you'd even blame me, and possibly even grow restless and want a divorce."

Lauren hung her head in despair. "Oh, Morgan, that would have never happened."

Morgan's grip loosened, and his thumbs came out to gently rub the back of her hands. "It does happen, Lauren. Especially in young marriages."

She lifted her head. "Maybe some young women do need that time, Morgan. But I didn't. I only wanted you and the life we could experience together."

His eyes were suddenly shadowed. "Instead you've had the burden of raising a child on your own. It wasn't what I—"

"Oh, my God! Scott!" Lauren gasped as it dawned on her that the whistle had ceased to blow.

Her head twisted in a desperate search for the child. But before she had the chance to panic in earnest, Morgan said, "There he is, on the picnic table."

Lauren let out a relieved breath and rose to see Scott sprawled on his back on the concrete table. It was obvious that the child was sound asleep.

Morgan followed as Lauren went to check on him. "It's just about his nap time," she told Morgan, "and when Scott gets sleepy he lies down wherever it's convenient for him."

"My kind of boy," Morgan said in amusement as they looked down at the contented child.

Scott had gone to sleep clutching the whistle Morgan had made for him, but the relaxed state of slumber had loosened the child's fingers around it. Tears smarted at the back of Lauren's eyes as she gently removed it.

This was Morgan's child, but he didn't know it. After everything he's just told her, would he want to know? Was he trying to tell her that he'd loved her all along? That he did care? Could she dare trust him again, especially now that Scott was involved?

Forcing the questions aside, she asked Morgan, "Would you care to lift him onto the pickup seat? I'm afraid the breeze here might be too cool for him."

"I'd be glad to," he told her.

Lauren went to open the pickup door while Morgan's strong arms lifted the sleeping boy. When they had him settled, warm and snug, on the pickup seat, Morgan asked, "How long will he sleep?"

His question reminded Lauren that even though he'd fathered Scott, Morgan knew nothing about the habits of babies and young children. "Usually about an hour. I imagine all this fresh air and exercise has done him in."

Morgan took her by the hand. "Why don't we walk down to the stream? The pickup will still be in sight if Scott happens to wake up."

"All right," she agreed.

Morgan's hand remained in hers, and Lauren wondered why even this simple contact with him could draw a physical response from her, from her head to her toes. He had too powerful an effect on her. But then, he always had.

The ground was cool and damp, so they chose to sit on a fallen pine that had long ago lost its bark. The wood was bleached and worn by the elements. Morgan ran his big hand over the trunk and commented, "Wasted lumber."

Lauren chuckled. "Spoken like a true miller." She cocked her head sideways to look at him. "Are you happy running the mill, Morgan?"

He lifted his head to the sky, and Lauren took the liberty of eyeing his strong profile against the azure background. Morgan's face was roughly hewn. Together with his lean but muscular build, his looks made women turn their heads with an appreciative "Oh." Lauren knew it was his sex appeal that drew their attention.

She felt the attraction even now and wondered why she seemed to have no defense against it.

"I never expected to take over the whole thing at this point in my life. Dad's passing was a jolt."

"I'm sure it must have been. I'm really sorry he was taken from you, Morgan. But if I know Mr. Sinclair, he's very pleased that you're handling things in the right way."

He slanted her an inquisitive look. "How do you know I'm handling things right?"

She shrugged, then smiled, and Morgan watched the slow movement of her lips. "I just know you are. You always were too smart for your own britches. And you couldn't be driving that extravagant Lincoln if you weren't handling things the right way."

He chuckled, then said, "Clever girl."

"So, are you happy running the mill?" she asked, coming back to her initial question.

"Hmm... Yes, I like it," he replied lazily. "I wouldn't want to do anything else."

"You were always good with numbers. You could have been an accountant."

He snorted with laughter at Lauren's statement. "I can only stand being behind walls for a short period of time. And I'd never surrender to wearing horn-rimmed glasses."

She laughed softly. "Do all accountants wear horn-rimmed glasses?"

He grinned and slid his hands down his long legs, which were stretched out in front of him. "I thought they did."

"Well, I'd rather think you like being a miller because you're the boss, and you always did have a bossy mouth."

A saucy glint appeared in his eyes. "You think so, huh?"

"Most definitely," she said with smug confidence.

He leaned closer, his eyes smiling, taunting her.

Lauren was in trouble. She knew it the minute her eyes slipped to the object of their discussion. "I—I know it has a habit of talking when it should be quiet," she whispered.

Lauren saw his brows rise in surprise. Then everything was blocked out as his face drew down to hers.

"I remember everything about your mouth, Lauren," he murmured. "How sweet it is…how responsive…how much I've wanted to feel it again."

His warm breath against her cheeks was an aphrodisiac. Slowly her eyelids drooped until her black lashes were dark, crescent-shaped fans against her cheeks. Morgan brushed his lips against both lids, then down her nose.

Lauren was giddy by the time his mouth reached hers, and she shuddered when he took her upper lip between his. The consequences failed to enter her mind. Unwittingly, her fingers curved against his chest and her mouth opened for him.

Lauren's response elicited a deep-seated hunger within Morgan. His hands reached blindly. One plunged into her hair, and the other captured her shoulder.

He tugged her close and she didn't resist. She willingly pressed herself against him, knowing that in his arms she'd find that old familiar feeling she'd missed so badly these past four years.

Like a flower reaching for the sun, her hands lifted and cupped his face. His fingers threaded deep into her hair until they were pressed against the nape of her neck, holding her fast.

By the time the kiss ended, Lauren's eyes were dazed. Morgan's were blazing. "Morgan, this isn't wise," she said in a breathy whisper. "It's reckless and—"

"I tried to be wise once, Lauren," he said, his nose nuzzling her cheek, "and I wound up losing you. And right now, being reckless feels good—damn good."

She started to speak but could utter no more than a gasp as his hands moved over the small mounds of her breasts. The nipples reacted with painful pleasure, hardening instantly against his palms.

As if Morgan already knew what she wanted, his hands searched for the hem of her sweater, then slid eagerly beneath it. Lauren was completely lost, her senses spinning out of control, when his fingers found the object of their desire.

She groaned with abandon and Morgan responded to the need in her voice by claiming her lips once again. His tongue thrust possessively between her teeth to fuel the heat already building inside her.

It was sinful how much she wanted him. Sinful, delicious and dangerous! In spite of all that had happened, in spite of the hurt, Lauren knew that all he had to do was lay her back on the cool bed of leaves and she would gladly give him his heart's desire.

Beneath Morgan's hands, her breasts were warm satin, the firm thrust filling no more than his palms. Her mouth was open, hungry and inviting. And suddenly all his thoughts catapulted back in time. He was making love to her all over again. Her thighs were bare and soft against his. Her cries of love were in his ear, her lips were on his neck, his cheeks, his chest, his mouth. She was his for the loving. For all time.

Morgan's breath was short and grating raspily in his throat as he tried to shake himself from the grip of passion. The two of them weren't alone. Scott was only a few yards away—asleep, but nevertheless there. Morgan couldn't make love to her now, even though his body was screaming for the privilege.

With the last of his self-control threatening to cave in, Morgan thrust Lauren away from him, turned his head and drew in yet another lungful of air.

Lauren was slow in coming down to earth. Reluctantly she opened her eyes and struggled to pull her shaken senses back together.

"I'm sorry, Lauren," Morgan finally said. He fumbled with a pack of cigarettes in his pocket, lit one, then said, "For a few moments I forgot Scott was here with us."

Even now Lauren had the urge to close her eyes and reach for him again. She was crazy to want him, and she knew it. But it seemed there wasn't any way to cure herself of it.

"Yes, well, maybe we should be thankful he is here. It kept us from doing something we'd both regret."

At her words, Morgan's head snapped around, his eyes narrowed to slits. "A moment ago you didn't act so regretful."

She groaned helplessly and looked away from him. "No, I don't regret what happened just now," she said honestly. "But I would if we'd—"

"If we'd made love," he finished for her in a voice that held some of the frustration he was feeling.

"Yes," she answered hoarsely.

"Why? Did you regret making love with me four years ago?"

The question punctured Lauren's heart. Slowly she turned to face him. "Yes. I did regret it. But only because it tore us apart."

Morgan studied her with such intensity that Lauren shivered. "If you hadn't left for Houston I would've ended up making love to you again and again, even though it would have been taking advantage of your love for me. That's how much I wanted you."

Didn't he know that she'd wanted him just as badly? "I—I thought you'd stopped wanting me after—after that night."

Groaning, he reached out and pulled her head into the curve of his shoulder. "Never," he said simply, stroking the top of her hair. "I still want you."

Resting her cheek against his collarbone, she slanted her eyes up to his face. "And I want you, Morgan. I won't deny that. But this is all too sudden.

We hurt each other in the past. I don't want us to repeat that mistake.''

"You'll only be here for another week.''

Did he really care? Was he trying to say he'd miss her? It was impossible to keep the light of hope from creeping into her heart.

"And I'd like to spend part of it with you, if you'd like that, too,'' she whispered.

His fingers meshed in her curls and rubbed gently against her scalp. "What makes you think I wouldn't?''

"Because in all the time I was away, you never tried to get in touch with me. All you had to do was ask my mother and she would have told you my address.''

Lauren's voice had grown a little testy, but Morgan didn't mind. In her own way, she was letting him know she'd wanted to hear from him. And at the moment that was all he needed to hear.

"At first, I didn't contact you because I was afraid you'd misconstrue it as an encouragement to come back. Then, after a lengthy amount of time passed and I didn't hear anything from you, I figured you'd either outgrown me or forgotten me entirely.''

Lauren was overwhelmed by what he was saying. It contradicted everything she'd believed these past years. "You mean *you* wanted to hear from *me*?'' she asked carefully.

He groaned, as if he couldn't believe she was even asking the question. "I prayed to hear from you,'' he said.

Pushing away from his chest, she looked at him in astonishment. He couldn't know the agonizing regret she felt at this moment. "Oh, Morgan," she whispered.

His face was grave as he said, "I needed to know what you were doing, if you were all right. That you were still thinking of me, that you still loved me. I wanted to tell you that I'd be waiting when the time was right for you to come home. But the only thing I ever got was the bits and pieces of information that Eileen gave me."

"I didn't know," Lauren said, her voice thick.

He sighed and reached out to smooth his thumb across her cheek. "No, I don't guess you did," he said ruefully. "You found someone else and—"

In that moment Lauren knew she could not let him go on thinking she'd been involved with another man and had borne his child. She had to let Morgan know that he was the only man she could ever make love to. If everything he said was true, surely he would welcome Scott.

"Morgan, there's something—"

Her words were suddenly halted when Scott's voice sounded from the pickup.

"Mama! Mama!"

Shakily she turned to look up the hill. Scott was leaning his head out the window, a big smile on his face.

"I went to sleep," he announced. Then he asked, "Can I get out now, Mama?"

From the wry smile on Morgan's face, she could

tell he wasn't nearly as frustrated with Scott's untimely wakening as she was.

"I think Scott thinks we've caged him," Morgan
said in amusement. Getting to his feet, he reached for
Lauren's hand. "We'd better go get him."

Lauren allowed him to pull her to her feet, and the
two of them started back up the slope. She told herself
that it was probably for the best that she hadn't
blurted out the truth a moment ago. They needed to
be alone and without distractions when she gave him
the news.

Eileen had gone on a shopping trip with an old
friend and wouldn't be back home until tonight. Lauren decided that when her mother returned she'd ask
her to watch Scott so that she and Morgan could go
somewhere and talk.

Lauren knew that telling Morgan about his son
would mean taking a frightening step into the future,
but now that she'd spent this time with him she felt
sure it was the right thing to do.

On the way home Morgan stopped at Queen Wilhelmina Park so that Scott could look over the little
zoo and ride the train. As Morgan had predicted, there
was still plenty of food left, and before they left the
park the three of them ate again.

While Morgan drove them down out of the mountains and toward home, Scott sat, drowsy and content,
with his head nestled against his mother's arm. Morgan talked about superficial things, and Lauren asked
him about the many people they both knew. As he
told her about several things that had happened in the

area, Lauren felt as if she'd been away a lifetime instead of only four years. It was going to be hard for her to leave home again, particularly now that she and Morgan had made a peace of sorts.

Eileen was still out when Morgan parked the pickup in front of the Magee house. Lauren was disappointed. Now that she'd firmly made up her mind to tell him about Scott, she didn't want to delay it any longer.

Morgan carried Lauren's picnic basket while she herded Scott up the steps and into the house.

"Looks like Mother is still out shopping," she told Morgan. "Buying Christmas presents, I expect. She'll probably make Scott and me leave the room when she brings in the packages."

Morgan wondered if Lauren was planning to come back to Mena for Christmas. He even opened his mouth to ask her, but then promptly closed it.

To hell with asking her. He wasn't going to let her go back to Houston—now or ever. Just when he'd decided this, he didn't know. Maybe, subconsciously, that first day he'd seen her, he'd known he had to have her back in his life.

"It is getting closer to the holidays," he replied, following her into the kitchen with Scott trailing behind him.

Morgan hefted the basket onto the cabinet counter so that Lauren could stash away the leftovers. Scott called out, "I'm thirsty, Mama. Can I have orange juice?"

Lauren turned to look at the boy. "Okay, but

you've got to be washed up first. There's dirt all over you. Let Mama put the food away and then I'll take you to the bathroom.''

Before Scott could protest, Morgan said, "I'll take Scott and help him wash. You go on with what you're doing.''

Surprised but pleased by the offer, Lauren said, ''If you're sure, Morgan. But I can do it in just a minute or two.''

Morgan looked down at Scott who'd already sidled up against his leg. Winking at the boy, he said, "Me and Scott are buddies, aren't we, Scott?''

"Yep, we're buddies, Mama!'' Scott proudly announced and Lauren smiled, noticing he was still holding the wooden whistle. More than likely, he'd insist on taking it to bed with him tonight. In no time at all Scott had become attached to Morgan. She only hoped that her son wouldn't be hurt by it.

"Then you'd better behave in the bathroom and not splash water all over Morgan. Or he might scobb your knob.''

Giggling loudly, Scott plastered both hands over his curly black head. "No, he won't, Mama!'' he said confidently, then took off in a run toward the bathroom.

Morgan looked at Lauren and laughed. "I think he trusts me.''

Lauren smiled back at him. "Don't let him fool you. After he gets to know you, he'll test you just to see if you *will* scobb his knob.''

Morgan continued to chuckle as he started out of

the room. "I don't believe that for a minute. He's a little boy, and I know for a fact that little boys are never naughty."

Lauren's answering laughter followed him down the hall and brought a faint smile to Morgan's lips. He wished Eileen would show up soon. He wanted to get Lauren alone somewhere so he could tell her how he felt, so he could ask her to marry him.

Morgan knew that it was probably too soon, that he would probably be pushing her, but he wasn't going to let that stop him. He loved Lauren, and he'd gone through the hell of losing her once. He didn't intend to let it happen again.

Scott had already filled the bathroom sink to a dangerous level and squirted in a hefty amount of liquid soap by the time Morgan entered the small room.

"Mama always sets me up on the sink," Scott said, looking up at Morgan's towering frame.

"Oh, she does, does she? Well, we'd better do what your mama does. We don't want to mess up anything here," Morgan said, and reached for the boy to set him up on one side of the vanity.

Scott immediately raised his arms straight up over his head. It took Morgan a moment to realize that the child expected him to peel off his dirty T-shirt.

Having done that, Morgan glanced around the room for a washcloth. He located one in a vanity drawer and tossed it into the sink. The water Scott had run was barely lukewarm, so Morgan pulled the plug on half of it, then refilled the sink with hot water.

"What does your mama wash first?" Morgan asked.

Scott screwed up his face. "My face. Yuk! She says my hands are nasty. She saves them for last."

Morgan tried not to smile at that as he wrung out the warm cloth and proceeded to wipe the boy's grubby face. Being around children was totally new to Morgan, but as he looked at Scott he realized it was something he would enjoy with a passion.

When he'd first heard Scott call Lauren his mama he'd felt as if he'd been stabbed in the heart. He'd always believed he would be the father of Lauren's children. He'd been the first one to make love to her. By rights, Scott should belong to him and—

Morgan's mind screeched to a sudden halt. *He'd been the first to make love to her!* Scott couldn't be— No, he couldn't be *his*, could he?

Just the idea made Morgan tremble inside. He wiped Scott's face with gentle but absent strokes while his mind went into double overdrive.

No, he told himself once again. Lauren wouldn't do something like that! She'd been young and hurt back then, but she'd never have been that spiteful. *Lauren has always been full of compassion. She wouldn't keep your own child from you for three or—*

"Scott, can you tell me how old you are?"

Scott grinned, making his baby-plump cheeks dimple. "I'm almost three," he said proudly, holding up three dirt-smeared fingers.

"Boy, that's getting to be pretty big. When's your birthday?"

"January twentieth," he promptly replied.

Morgan took a deep breath and reached out to rinse the cloth in the water. That meant he was born nine months after Lauren left Mena!

God, why hadn't he thought of it before? It all fit, but he hadn't stopped to look at all the pieces. Everything made sense now. Lauren's suddenly leaving town and never coming back—not even for visits. Eileen's vague comments about Lauren. And now Lauren suddenly showing up here with a child and not being married.

Oh, God! Was this child really his? He rubbed his fingers along Scott's square little jaw, then glanced up in the mirror at his own face. Was there anything about Scott that resembled himself?

Tossing the cloth aside, he took Scott's face in both his hands and looked at the child with new eyes. As the moments passed, Morgan felt a sickness spread in his stomach and rise up to smother him.

The faint little crook of his nose was there in Scott's, as was the indentation of his chin, the shape of his jaw. Even Scott's complexion had the same warm golden color of Morgan's and not the ivory tones of his mother's.

"Can't you get the dirt off?" Scott asked.

The child's voice broke into Morgan's silent search. He dropped his hands from Scott's face and reached blindly for the washcloth. This was his child!

He was Scott's father! How could Lauren have done this to him?

The shattering realization was like a kick in the gut. He felt winded, and anger was pumping the blood through his veins with a vengeance.

"It's okay, I got the dirt off," Morgan told him, struggling to keep his voice and his expression normal. "Now let's do your hands, and then we'll get you a clean shirt."

Scott refused to relinquish his whistle, so Morgan allowed him to hold it in one hand while he washed the other.

It dawned on Morgan that the whittled toy was the first gift he'd given his son. The whole idea filled him with such a deep and sudden sense of loss that he had to fight the urge to clutch the boy fiercely to his breast and never let go.

Back in the kitchen, Lauren poured Scott a glass of orange juice, then glanced over to see if the coffee was finished dripping. It was, so she filled two cups and put them on a tray along with the orange juice. She carried it over to the kitchen table.

Morgan and Scott certainly were taking a long time getting washed up, she thought. She'd heard the mumble of their voices earlier, but now she couldn't hear a sound. No doubt Scott was teaching Morgan all about taking a sponge bath, she thought wryly.

Footsteps sounded in the doorway. Smiling, Lauren looked up to greet the two of them.

Morgan stood silhouetted in the door, and one

glance at his white face told Lauren something was terribly wrong.

"What happened?" she cried. "Where's Scott?"

The child's dark head suddenly bobbed out from behind Morgan's legs.

"I'm here, Mama," he said happily, reaching up to curl his little fingers around Morgan's big hand.

Lauren let out a relieved breath. But her relief was short-lived, as Morgan said in a deadly level voice, "And this is where my son is going to stay from now on, Lauren. With me."

Chapter Eight

The blood drained from Lauren's face, and her legs grew dangerously weak. The room tilted, and she grabbed at the edge of the table.

"Morgan," she said faintly.

His eyes were narrowed to two condemning slits, and Lauren was positive that granite couldn't be any harder than the set of his jaw.

She didn't know how or what had prompted him to put two and two together and come to the conclusion that Scott was his son. But it was too late to matter. The one thing Lauren knew was that the timing couldn't have been more rotten!

Unaware that anything unusual was taking place, Scott scrambled up on a chair and reached for his orange juice.

With slow, purposeful steps, Morgan walked into the kitchen and took a clenched hold on Lauren's arm.

"Come into the living room while Scott drinks his juice," he said in a tight, low voice.

She gave one jerky nod and loosened her grip on the table. Her legs were rubbery as he led her out of the room. Lauren was certain that if his hand hadn't been on her arm her legs would have given away.

"Morgan," she said once they were in the living room away from Scott, "I know this must be a shock for you, but—"

He spit out a curse that made her cringe. "A *shock*," he said mockingly. "A shock couldn't begin to describe how I feel!"

Swallowing, she pulled her arm out of his grasp and backed away from him. Thumping into the back of a chair, she grabbed at the stuffed arm for support.

Stricken, she whispered, "I didn't mean for you to find out this way."

His eyes blazed at her, and his lips twisted to a sneer. "Apparently you didn't mean for me to ever find out that I had a son!"

She winced at the condemnation in his voice. "That's not true! Scott is the reason I came back to Mena. I came back to tell you about him."

He took a few steps toward her, then halted, leaving only a couple of feet between them. His anger was a tangible thing, radiating out at her, washing her with fear. "I'll never believe that, Lauren," he said, gritting his teeth. "A person who deliberately keeps a child from his father would lie about anything."

Anger spurted through Lauren, replacing some of

her fear. "I didn't deliberately keep Scott from you," she said angrily.

The corner of his mouth lifted. "Then what would you call it, Lauren?"

She ignored the question. "You didn't want me. Why would you have wanted a child of mine?"

Morgan couldn't believe her. He couldn't believe any of this was happening. Blood pounded at his temples, and he had the desperate urge to break something with his bare hands.

"Because he's my child, too! He's my flesh and blood, Lauren. Just like you. And where in hell do you come off playing God?"

Two spots of red flamed in her paper-white face. "I wasn't playing at anything, Morgan! You didn't want to marry me, remember? You discarded me as if I were some dog you'd grown tired of tagging behind you. Why don't you face it? You didn't give a damn whether you'd gotten me pregnant or not."

"Lauren—"

"I was a virgin," she stormed. "You used no precautions. You're a smart man, Morgan. You knew the risks, but did you bother yourself to see if I was all right, physically or mentally?"

The only response from Morgan was the paleness spreading across his face.

Lauren answered her question for him. "No, you didn't. So you tell me, Morgan, does that sound like a man who wants to know he has a child?"

"Don't think you can twist things around to make

it look like you were the victim," he bit out. "It won't work, Lauren."

Her eyes grew hard. "No, nothing works between us. It never did. But that's easy to figure out, isn't it. I'm a hillbilly Magee. Something Sinclairs merely wipe their feet on." She laughed harshly, then said, "I must have been out of my mind to think bringing Scott back home was the right thing to do. You're just as callous now as you ever were! And as far as I'm concerned you'll never be a father to Scott!"

His angry eyes stabbed at her as he turned on his heel and started out the door. "Tell my son I'll see him tomorrow," he said coldly. Then he closed the door behind him.

Lauren didn't move until she heard the sound of Morgan's truck pull away, and by then she was shaking uncontrollably.

What did he mean? What did he intend to do? Oh, God, he couldn't take Scott from her, could he?

"Lauren, darling, what's the matter? Didn't the picnic with Morgan go well?"

Lauren was lying across the four-poster bed, where she'd been for the past hour. Her mother had come home sometime before that, happy and chattering about her day's outing. Lauren had been unable to tell her about Morgan, and the strain of pretending nothing was wrong was taking a heavy toll of her emotions.

Eileen came farther into the bedroom and dropped

down on the dressing bench. Lauren rolled onto her back and looked at her mother.

"The picnic was very nice. I enjoyed it more than I'd ever expected to, and Scott had a wonderful time."

"Then why are you hiding in the bedroom?"

Lauren closed her eyes and sighed. "Oh, Mama, Morgan found out about Scott," she said.

"Found out? You mean you told him?"

Her eyes still closed, Lauren shook her head. "No. He figured it out on his own."

Eileen let out a heavy sigh. "Well, I'm not surprised. Morgan isn't dumb. When you showed up with Scott he was bound to start counting." She studied Lauren's dejected face. "So what did he say? How did he take the news?"

Lauren groaned. "He was furious, to say the least."

Eileen's expression remained unmoved, as though she wasn't a bit surprised by the news. "What did you expect, Lauren? Flowers and thank-yous?"

Lauren gave her mother a surprised look. She'd never talked to her like this before. "Mama, you don't understand. Morgan wasn't just mad. He was…he was…" She swallowed and shook her head. "I don't know what he'll do—"

Pushing herself up on one arm, she looked desperately at her mother for some hint of reassurance. "He can't take Scott from me, can he, Mama? I mean, we're not married— He has no legal rights!"

Eileen passed a hand over her forehead. "I think

the law about that kind of thing has changed in the last few years. More and more unmarried men are winning custody of their children. Why? What did he do, threaten you with a court case?''

Lauren shook her head as she told herself not to panic. "Not in so many words, but—he plans to take Scott somehow. I have a feeling—''

Seeing the distress in her daughter's face, Eileen said soothingly, "Don't jump to wild conclusions, darling.'' She rose from the stool and sat down on the edge of the mattress next to her daughter. "Right now Morgan is hurt and angry. He probably said a lot of things he didn't really mean. So don't worry. He'll do the right thing about all this. Trust me.''

Lauren couldn't believe her mother's cool reaction. She flopped hopelessly back against the mattress and pressed the heels of her hands against her eyelids. "Right now I don't even know what the right thing is,'' she muttered miserably.

A moment passed. Then Eileen asked, "What were you hoping for, Lauren, when you first came back home?''

Lauren pulled her hands away from her eyes and looked at her mother. "I was hoping that Morgan would accept Scott as his son, maybe not with jubilance, but not—not with anger! And I wanted Scott to know his father, even if they couldn't be together on a day-to-day basis.'' She felt the warning of tears stinging the back of her eyes, forcing her to close her lids before her mother could spot them. "Mama, everything was going so well today. Morgan was so wonderful with Scott and—and he even intimated that he wanted to put our past differences behind us and start over again. But…but then he realized Scott was his before I had a chance to tell him and…and everything was ruined.…"

Lauren's voice faded to a tremulous whisper that had Eileen shaking her head. "I expect he feels you betrayed him by keeping Scott a secret."

Everything inside Lauren suddenly hardened, and she opened her misty eyes. "And how do you think I felt when he told me to get out of his life?"

Eileen didn't answer her daughter. Instead, she sat studying her with a serious expression. "That's behind you now, Lauren. You should be thinking about Scott and his future, not hating Morgan for rejecting you in the past."

Lauren dropped her chin and stared unseeingly at the print on the patchwork quilt. "I know, Mama, I know. But every time I'm with Morgan I get so—"

When Lauren couldn't go on, Eileen reached over and patted her daughter's arm. "I know, honey. And I also know that if you really try you can work all of this out. Morgan is a compassionate man. He won't deliberately do anything to hurt you or his son."

"Mother, you think you know Morgan, but you don't. I keep telling you, he's a Sinclair. They don't do the right thing where people like us are concerned."

Eileen's lips compressed to a tight line. "You might have loved Morgan, Lauren. But I don't think you ever understood him." She rose from the bed and walked over to the door, then looked back at Lauren's stricken face. "I tried to warn you about this before Scott was born," she said. "But you didn't want Morgan to marry you under those conditions. I can't blame you for that, Lauren. But now I'm wondering if those terms wouldn't have been better than what you're facing now."

Later that night, Lauren was preparing for bed when the telephone rang. The hairbrush she'd been about to pull through her hair stopped in midair as she waited for her mother to answer the call. Could it be Morgan? Was he calling to tell her he'd already decided to take legal action?

The thought was so abhorrent that she refused to consider it. In spite of everything, she loved Morgan. Her heart refused to see any of the pain, the threats, the accusations. All it could see was him.

"Lauren...telephone."

Her mother's voice jarred her back to awareness. With a shaky hand she laid the hairbrush on the dresser, glanced at Scott's sleeping figure in the bed, then hurried out the door.

Eileen didn't have to tell her it was Morgan. Lauren could see it in her face as the other woman handed her the receiver.

Once her mother had left the room, Lauren said, "Hello." Her throat knotted on just that one word. She swallowed convulsively as she waited for him to respond.

"Lauren, I want to see you in the morning. Alone.

Can Eileen watch Scott?'' His voice was cold, crisp and impersonal.

"Mama will be at work."

There was a brief silence. Then Morgan said, "He can stay with Mother. After all, Scott needs to know he has another grandmother."

She hadn't even stopped to think about Mrs. Sinclair! "Morgan, have you—have you told your mother about Scott?"

"Yes. Why? Were you planning on me waiting three or four years?"

Lauren gritted her teeth. "Maybe I deserve every hateful thing you say, Morgan. But right now I think we'd both do better to focus our attention on Scott."

"Scott is the *only* thing I'm concerned about," he assured her in a brittle tone, "and I'd advise you not to even consider running back to Houston, if that idea has been traipsing through your mind."

Stung, Lauren felt a powerful urge to slam the receiver down. She took a deep breath in an effort to calm herself. "I tried to tell you earlier, Morgan, that I came back to Mena solely for the purpose of telling you about Scott. It would be rather pointless to leave now, wouldn't it?"

"I'm not interested in any of your lies," he said, making Lauren catch her breath painfully. "Just be over here in the morning. Early."

"I'll be there," she replied stiffly. Her hand was aching, and she suddenly realized she had a stranglehold on the telephone receiver. "With Scott," she added.

"Oh, and just to give you something to sleep on—You've had Scott for three years. I've decided it's my turn now."

"Morgan!"

Before his name was completely out, the click in her ear told her he'd hung up. For a moment she considered calling him back. But the sensible side of her made her set the receiver back in its cradle.

Calling Morgan would be pointless. He was out for vengeance, and nothing was going to stop him.

It was raining the next morning when Lauren and Scott drove over the winding gravel road to Morgan's place. Fog shrouded the distant mountains, and water dripped from the tall green pines growing at the edge of the road.

The dreary weather was fitting, Lauren thought. It should be cold and rainy on a day of retribution.

Lauren had slept little, if at all. Her eyes felt puffy, and she knew the dark circles beneath them didn't help her appearance any.

But her looks were the last thing worrying her at the moment, and she knew it showed in the white shirt and faded jeans she'd hurriedly pulled on this morning.

"Mama, will Morgan take us on another picnic today?" Scott asked, his little nose pressed against the foggy window.

Lauren suddenly felt the need to weep for everything she'd had in the past with Morgan and everything she and Scott wouldn't have with him in the future.

"I'm afraid not, darling," she managed to say after a while. "It's raining today, and we'd get all wet. Even the squirrels are in their holes today."

Surprisingly, Sylvia, Morgan's mother, answered the door. She was a statuesque woman with faded blond hair that she wore in a soft French twist. Even before she'd gone to Houston, Lauren had barely known the woman. Morgan had invited Lauren to his home only rarely. She'd gotten the idea that Sylvia Sinclair didn't approve of her son's associating with someone like Lauren.

The idea that Morgan's mother didn't think Lauren was good enough for her son had not really bothered Lauren back then. She'd been so much in love with Morgan that she'd been confident nothing could keep them apart—certainly not his socialite mother. But now, standing face-to-face with Sylvia, Lauren wondered what the older woman was thinking about her. That she'd come back to deliberately trap her son?

"Come in," Sylvia said, pushing the door aside for Lauren and Scott to enter.

Morgan was sitting on a long tweed couch pushed against one wall of the wide room. Scott ran straight to him and climbed up on his lap.

"I brought my whistle, Morgan. See?"

Morgan's face held a gentle smile for Scott. Lauren felt a great sense of loss as she watched Morgan's reaction to their son. He would never look at her with tenderness again, and all because she'd loved him too much to force him into marrying her out of a sense of duty.

"Yes, I do see," Morgan said.

"Can I blow it in your house?"

Morgan chuckled at the question. "Sure you can. Blow it and see if it still works."

Scott didn't hesitate to show Morgan that the whistle did indeed still work. While he blew on it, Sylvia turned to Lauren, who was still standing awkwardly in the middle of the room.

"Would you like coffee or juice, Lauren?"

Lauren shook her head. "No, thank you, Mrs. Sinclair. Scott and I just finished breakfast."

She nodded and motioned for Lauren to take a seat. "Please make yourself comfortable," she said as if she were the hostess of an afternoon tea instead of a woman seeing her grandchild for the first time.

Lauren silently wondered if Sylvia doubted Scott's parentage. Perhaps she believed Lauren was making up the whole thing in an effort to get to the Sinclair money.

That was certainly a hilarious idea, Lauren thought. Money was the last thing she'd ever wanted from Morgan. In fact, she'd often wished he didn't have any.

Although Lauren took a seat in an armchair opposite Morgan and Scott, Sylvia didn't seat herself. She walked over to Scott and bent to touch his curly black hair.

The child looked up at her. "What's your name?" he asked guilelessly.

Sylvia laughed good-naturedly. "My name is Sylvia," she told him. "I'm Morgan's mother."

Scott looked at the tall woman, then back to Morgan, as if to confirm her statement.

"Would you like to walk down to my house, Scott, and take a look at an aquarium? It's full of pretty fish. We'll take an umbrella so it won't rain on us."

Uncertain, Scott looked at his mother. Lauren nodded. "It's okay, honey. You may go with Morgan's mother if you'd like."

Obviously deciding the fish were too tempting to pass up, he climbed down from Morgan's lap and went along with Sylvia.

"'Bye, Mama. I'm gonna go look at the fish!"

"See you later, honey," Lauren said.

As the two of them started out the door, Morgan told his mother, "We'll be down to get him later on."

Sylvia nodded and shut the door behind them. There was a wide window overlooking the porch. Lauren watched the two of them as the woman opened a bright red umbrella. She could hear Scott talking as he and his grandmother started out across the lawn. A moment later, they disappeared behind a stand of pine trees. Then all was quiet. She and Morgan were alone.

Lauren let out a shaky breath and glanced across the room at him. He was looking at her with an impassive expression that made her feel cold inside.

Morgan gazed at the small, pale figure in the armchair. In spite of her age, Lauren still seemed little more than a child herself. It was incredible to think that she'd given birth to his son. A part of him felt terribly guilty and remorseful about that. But the bitter part of him said that she'd chosen to bear the burden of pregnancy alone. She hadn't loved him enough to want his help or his love. She hadn't even cared enough to let him know he had a son.

Lauren's clenched nerves knotted even tighter as she waited for him to speak. She wondered if he'd lain awake as she had last night.

Suddenly Morgan rose to his feet. Lauren's eyes resembled a tense, flightly doe's as they followed his movements. In spite of the cool, dreary morning, the room felt airless and hot to Lauren. She wished he would say what he planned to say and get it out in the open. Her self-control was stretched so thin that she knew it could snap at any time.

"You called me over here to talk, Morgan. What is it? Have you decided to take legal action against me? You think you can win a custody battle?"

He gave her a hard look, jammed his hands in the back pockets of his blue jeans and walked over to the patio doors that faced out on the backyard.

"I considered it," he said brusquely. "I believe a judge would be sympathetic to my case. Deliberately keeping a child from his other parent would be viewed as cruel any way you look at it."

She flinched at the cold anger in his voice.

"I'm not stupid, Morgan. I know I wouldn't stand a prayer in court against you, a Sinclair. Even if the judge didn't view my actions as cruel, you'd win simply because of your money and the fact that you could provide Scott with more monetarily.''

He glanced at her over his shoulder. ''I'm glad you realize that.''

She let out a harsh laugh. ''Realize what, Morgan? That I'm poor and you're rich? It's something I've never forgotten.'' Her chin jutted forward. ''Don't you think I know that none of this would have happened if I'd been like you?''

''Meaning what, Lauren?'' he asked wearily.

Her nostrils flared with sudden anger, and she had to stop herself from grasping both arms of the chair and digging her fingernails into the nubby upholstery. ''Meaning four years ago I was good enough to make love to, but not good enough to marry.''

For a long moment he stared at her, the expression on his face hard and unyielding. Then, abruptly, he turned back to the glass doors.

''You have a twisted sense of reality, Lauren.''

''Well, you've twisted more than just my senses, Morgan. So feel free to take all the credit for the change in me.''

Morgan winced inwardly at that, because he was afraid it was partly true. But, damn it, he hadn't known she was pregnant! It wouldn't have been like this if he'd known. And he wanted to hate her for that, for purposely hurting them both.

''I don't intend to take this to court, Lauren,'' he said. ''I don't want Scott's life marred by a custody battle.''

Lauren breathed a little easier. Maybe he wasn't

quite as heartless as she'd first thought. "Thank you for that much, Morgan," she said quietly. "Surely you know by now that Scott is my whole life. I only want what's best for him."

Morgan pulled his hands from his pockets and turned to face her. The twist of his lips mocked the love she still held in her heart for him.

"I'm glad you feel that way, Lauren, because I feel the same way, too. That's why I've decided the best thing for you and me to do is to get married."

It took a few seconds for his words to sink in. When they did, shock propelled her to her feet.

"Married!" she gasped.

"You have objections to that?" he asked, so impersonally that Lauren had to fight not to run at him and beat her fists against his broad chest.

"Yes, I do! If you marry me now, the last four years will have been pointless!"

Lauren went to stand before him, her eyes wild and dark, her fists clenched at her sides. She couldn't believe this was happening. It was her worst nightmare come true.

Morgan folded his big, golden-haired arms across his chest. "Am I supposed to understand that?"

"I didn't want you to marry me out of a sense of duty then. I don't want you doing it now! I won't do it. I simply won't!"

His eyes narrowed at her words. "If you want to be with your son, you will. Because as far as I'm concerned, that's the only alternative."

"What does that mean? That you'd simply take

him away from me? Are you that kind of man, Morgan?'' she asked in a stunned voice.

He let out a long breath and raked his hand through his hair, disheveling his rumpled curls even more. ''You're his mother, Lauren. And I happen to think that our son deserves two parents.''

She felt suddenly weak, and her knees quivered inside her jeans. ''So do I. But not like this!''

''If you're worried I'm marrying you because I feel obligated, then let me set you straight. The only reason I'm marrying you is so I can be with my son and give him the rightful name of Sinclair. As for you and me, well...'' he said dryly, ''I think we both know there's nothing to be salvaged from our past relationship.''

If Lauren's heart had been broken before, it was now falling into a myriad of tiny, shattered pieces. Unwittingly her eyes filled with pain as she looked up at his hard face. ''That's not what you hinted at yesterday,'' she said in a tremulous voice.

His brown eyes stabbed at her. ''Yesterday I thought I was seeing the old Lauren I loved, the Lauren who would never even have considered cheating me out of three years of my child's life. Today I know that woman is gone. She's the one I wanted. Not you.''

Morgan's words were like a knife wound to her heart. Numb, she turned away from him and crossed to the picture window at the front of the room. As she looked at the heavy rain, she was certain she was dying. No one could hurt like this and live.

The rain splashed against the broad brown sycamore leaves and filled the cracks and crevices on the
stone sidewalk. Fall had come to kill off all summer
life, and as the creeping chill settled in Lauren's heart
she knew that, like fall, Morgan was taking all the
life from her.

"Then I take it that ours will be a marriage of
convenience only?" she asked after long minutes had
stretched by.

"You deceived me in a cruel, heartless way, Lauren. Do you honestly think I'd want to make love to
you?"

She heard his voice from across the room. It was
cold and distant, warning her that to turn and look at
him now would be both pointless and painful.

"And you must know I could never make love to
a man who took the most precious gift I had to give
and then cold-bloodedly turned away from me."

Morgan looked at her slumped shoulders with sad
eyes and wondered if, like him, she was lying to sal-
vage her pride.

Chapter Nine

Lauren and Morgan were married three days later. It was a quiet, simple ceremony performed in the judge's chambers with only Lauren's mother, Scott and Sylvia Sinclair accompanying them.

It was one of the saddest days in Lauren's life. She repeated the marriage vows with a heavy heart, knowing that it all meant nothing to Morgan. Whatever love he'd had for her in the past she'd managed to kill by keeping Scott's birth a secret. That was something she couldn't change, and she knew that her chances of a real marriage to Morgan were gone, too. Her wedding day wasn't anything like what she'd dreamed of and yearned for.

For the ceremony Lauren wore the same pink dress she'd worn the night Morgan had taken her to dinner. In the past, Morgan had often told her she looked pretty in pink with her black hair and pale skin, but she doubted he'd noticed today.

He barely glanced at her while the judge talked about the true meaning and sanctity of marriage. But he did give her a pink long-stemmed rose before the ceremony, and afterward he kissed her briefly on the lips. She supposed he did it merely for the sake of appearances.

Sighing heavily, Lauren turned away from the picture window. Four days had passed since then, but the memory was as fresh and painful as if it were yesterday.

Today had been a beautiful day, and now the fading late-afternoon sun was lengthening the shadows. Scott was playing outside, piling sycamore leaves into great mounds, then jumping into the spongy beds with a multitude of squeals and shouts. Morgan had a bird dog named Goldy, who was happy to have been presented with a playmate in Scott. In the four days since the wedding the boy and the dog had rarely been separated.

Scott seemed happy enough living here in Morgan's house. Several days ago they'd told the child that Morgan was his father, and he'd accepted the news readily. Lauren knew he was still too young to know what it all meant. He only knew that he now had a huge house to live in, a dog to play with and a big, tall man he could call his very own daddy.

It was enough that Scott was happy, Lauren thought as she walked through the living room and headed toward the kitchen. Scott was the whole rea-

son for this marriage, and if he was happy and ben-
efiting from it, she'd look on it as a success. That was
the only way she could survive Morgan's day-to-day
indifference.

Twenty to five, Lauren read from her watch. Morgan would be home from the mill in little less than
an hour, so she decided to go ahead and start the
vegetables and meat for supper.

The kitchen in Morgan's house was beautiful, and
during the past few days Lauren had discovered that
it was her favorite room in the house.

It was decorated in white and Wedgwood blue, and
the cabinets were made of varnished pine that had
been sawed at the Sinclair Mill. There was every kind
of modern convenience on hand, making cooking and
cleaning up hardly a job at all. Yet Lauren knew that
this was her favorite room because it was the only
place in the house where Morgan acknowledged her
personally. When the three of them gathered around
the table to eat, Lauren could almost think of them
as a real, loving family.

Breakfast and supper. Lauren lived for those two
times of the day. She watched the clock and decided
what she would cook. Marrying Morgan had reduced
her life to these two events, and she knew that was
not a good thing. But she was at a loss as to how to
solve the problem. Living with Morgan but not really
living with him was hurting her more than anything
she'd gone through over the past four years.

Lauren was just placing the last dish on the table
when she heard the slam of the front door, then the

muted sound of voices. A second later Scott burst into the kitchen, dirt on his hands and bits of broken leaves in his hair, smelling like a dog.

"Daddy's home, Mama! And he says he's hungry!"

"That's good," Lauren said, giving her son a tender smile. "So why don't you hurry to the bathroom and you can wash with him."

Scott didn't have to be told twice. He liked to be anywhere Morgan was.

The two of them appeared in the kitchen just as Lauren was placing their drinks on the table—milk for Scott and hot coffee for Lauren and Morgan.

Morgan watched her graceful movements with mixed emotions. He'd never expected it to be so hard to have her living under the same roof with him. When he'd discovered that Scott was his and that she'd kept that fact from him all this time, he'd expected to hate her for the rest of his life. But he'd found he couldn't hate her, even for one moment.

She'd accepted the terms without argument and for these past few days had strived to make the house into a pleasant home for the three of them. She'd been neither dry nor accusing. Nor had she been cloyingly sweet. In fact, if she would only smile and laugh, she would almost be the old Lauren. And Morgan couldn't deny—at least not to himself—that he looked forward to coming home and knowing that she and Scott would be waiting for him.

Each evening he'd find her in the kitchen, and smells of cooking would be filling the room. She'd be there in her old jeans, her black hair bushed around her face from all the extra humidity.

Morgan had never expected her to cook for him, or to do it with such a passion. He'd never expected her to look so beautiful or so desirable, and each day not touching her was becoming more and more of a struggle for him.

Morgan didn't want to want her. He didn't want to love her, and he fought against his feelings with everything inside him. But he found they held on, making him watch her with hungry eyes and hope she would never see, never know.

He said nothing to her as he took his place at the table. Scott climbed up into the chair beside him, picked up his fork and scraped the tines across the empty plate.

Lauren took her seat across from the two of them and reached for Scott's plate, avoiding Morgan's gaze.

"You should be hungry, young man. You and Goldy have run all day long."

She'd make chicken-fried steak from coarsely ground sirloin. On the side were mashed potatoes and tiny green peas in a cream sauce. She filled Scott's plate with some of each, then cut his meat into small, bite-size pieces.

"Me and Goldy piled the leaves in a big mountain," Scott told his father. "But then Goldy chased the ball into it and tore it all up."

Morgan smiled down at Scott and affectionately rumpled the top of his head. It was still amazing to know that this beautiful little boy was his, a product of the love he and Lauren had shared. He thought of that night almost every time he looked at Scott. And, despite everything, he knew he was glad it had happened. He was glad that Lauren had borne his child.

"So you and Goldy have been playing, eh? You didn't stray out of the yard and worry your mama, did you?"

Scott shook his head emphatically. "No, Daddy. I'm good. I'm not like Joey."

Lauren had to stifle a laugh when Morgan arched an inquisitive brow at her.

"Joey was our neighbor down in Houston. He was always doing naughty things, then blaming it on Scott," she explained. "One of his most notable was when he smeared mud all over Aunt Hattie's car windows."

"Sounds like a lovely child," he said dryly.

Lauren shrugged. "He just needed attention at home. I felt sorry for him. His parents were divorced, and neither one wanted him. His grandmother was raising him."

Morgan watched her ladle food onto her plate, thinking that she'd always been softhearted. She'd always loved every living thing as if God had made it just for her to enjoy. Still, he didn't understand how she could have nurtured, borne and lovingly raised his child and not wanted him to know. Had she hated him that much?

The question brought a hard set to Morgan's face, and he turned his attention back to his food.

"Speaking of Houston," Lauren went on, "I'm afraid I'm going to have to make a trip down there to get business straightened away at the salon. And there's also the matter of our clothes and things at Hattie's. Did you want me to take Scott or leave him here with you?"

His head jerked up sharply. "You're planning on going alone?"

Her green eyes widened with surprise. "Well, yes...I guess. Since Mama works, it would be hard for her to make the trip with me. But I did wonder if I could drive your pickup. I don't think I could get all our things packed into my little car."

She hated asking him for the truck. She'd have liked to remain as independent as possible, since he did not consider her a wife in the true sense. But it would be childish of her to fret about her pride at a time like this.

Morgan looked at her, his mind racing back and forth. He wanted to tell her to go on and leave Scott with him. That way he could be sure she'd come back. She wouldn't leave her baby for anything. But he didn't want to think of her driving those hundreds of miles alone. Anything could happen to her. On the other hand, he was afraid to let her take Scott. He was afraid he'd never see his son or his wife again.

She wasn't happy. He would have had to be blind not to see it. She hadn't wanted to marry him. He'd blackmailed her into it. She might decide that taking Scott and running away would be better than living with him.

"I'll take you to Houston, Lauren," he heard himself saying. "But it will have to be this weekend. I'll be tied up at the mill until then."

A strange fire shot through Lauren. He would take her to Houston himself! Stunned, she said, "I don't want to put you out, Morgan. It's a long, tiring trip. And you're so busy with the mill."

His eyes dropped to his food. God, he couldn't let her know how desperate he was to hold on to her. It was crazy, he knew, but he loved her. In spite of the way she'd hurt him, he still loved her. He couldn't let her know. He didn't even want to admit to himself that he could be so stupid.

"My foreman can watch over things."

Lauren didn't know what to think about his offer. She wanted to believe he wanted to be with her, and that he was concerned about her driving all that distance alone. But both of those reasons were highly unlikely. The only thing Morgan cared about was Scott. She just happened to be his son's mother, and that was all she meant to Morgan. That fact was something she was just going to have to learn to live with.

"Thank you, Morgan. I'll call Aunt Hattie tonight and let her know we'll be coming. She'll be happy to have our things packed and ready to go."

He nodded in acquiescence and Lauren turned her attention back to the food on her plate. But inside, her senses were whirling around like a tornado. Morgan was going with her to Houston, and no matter what his reasons were, she was happy about it.

* * *

To Lauren's relief, on Saturday the weather turned out to be beautiful, allowing them to travel under cloudless skies. As they drove deeper into Texas, it grew warmer and more humid. By the time they'd crossed the Sabine River, the two of them had both shed the jackets they'd started out with. When Houston loomed on the horizon, Lauren was wishing she'd worn shorts.

During the trip, Morgan didn't go out of his way to make conversation, although he did make scattered comments about the different landscape and climate. Lauren wasn't surprised by his cool attitude toward her. As far as she was concerned, since they'd been married he'd kept everything impersonal. In fact, if not for Scott, it would have been hard for anyone to tell that they'd ever shared anything in the past. Not love, laughter, friendship or the making of a child.

It was as if he'd wiped it all away and now saw her as someone he didn't know and didn't particularly want to know.

Lauren did her best not to dwell on that somber thought. Morgan did speak to her on his own initiative sometimes. Maybe someday his anger toward her would mellow and he'd be able to forgive her to some degree. It might be that he could then share his thoughts and time with her—maybe not as a husband, but at least as a friend. That was the most Lauren could hope for.

"So this is where you lived for the past four years?"

Morgan had just swung the pickup into the driveway of her aunt and uncle's modest home. Surprised by his question, she looked at him.

"Yes. Bob and Hattie treated me like their own daughter. I'll miss them," she said.

He grimaced as he switched off the motor. Was she already wishing she could divorce him? Was she wishing she hadn't left Houston in the first place?

Night had not yet fallen. They found Hattie in the backyard charcoaling hamburgers. She was wearing a brightly printed halter dress because of the heat. Her brown hair was twisted up at the back of her head and curled damply around her face. She was such a familiar and comforting sight that Lauren flew into her arms and cried softly on her shoulder.

Morgan stood to one side, watching the scene with a stiff expression and wondering for the first time if he'd made a mistake in forcing Lauren to marry him. He didn't want to hurt her, but he knew he was. He just couldn't seem to stop himself. There was so much pain inside him that he couldn't keep it from spilling over onto her.

"There, now, honey girl," Hattie murmured soothingly, holding Lauren away from her. "What are all these tears about?"

Afraid to glance at Morgan, Lauren merely sniffed and smiled at Hattie. "I'm just so happy to see you, that's all."

Hattie patted her cheek. "And I've missed you," she said. "But I'm anxious to meet this new husband of yours."

Lauren pulled out of Hattie's embrace. Taking her aunt by the arm, she led her over to Morgan.

He was dressed in jeans and boots and a blue shirt with the sleeves rolled back on his forearms. He looked big and tall and handsome, even by Texas standards. Lauren knew her aunt was silently overwhelmed by Morgan's masculine presence.

"Hello, Mrs. Sawyer," he said, extending his hand to Hattie.

"It's nice to meet you, Morgan. May I call you Morgan?"

"I'd be honored," he said warmly, taking her offered hand.

Lauren watched the two of them from beneath lowered lashes, wondering if Morgan's voice would ever have any warmth in it for her.

"And please—I'm Hattie to everyone," her aunt insisted.

The sound of meat sizzling suddenly caught the older woman's attention. She hurried back to the charcoal grill.

"I hope you two are hungry. Nothing fancy—just hamburgers, potato salad and cheesecake. I'm sorry to say Bob will be working this evening. Maybe you'll have a chance to meet him in the morning before you leave."

"You shouldn't have gone to all this trouble, Hattie," Morgan told her. "Lauren and I could have gone out to eat."

Hattie gave him a horrified look. "I wouldn't have heard of it. Sending my new nephew out to eat! Now wouldn't that have been something," she said with a cluck of her tongue. Then she looked questioningly at Lauren. "Where's Scott?"

"He stayed with Mama. There wasn't any sense in dragging him along and wearing him out with such a long drive."

"Oh." She sighed with disappointment. "I miss my little boy. I was looking forward to seeing him. But I guess it's Eileen's turn to have her grandson now."

The three of them talked for a few more minutes, and then Hattie sent them into the house to wash. By the time Lauren and Morgan returned to the patio, Hattie had everything ready and on the table.

"It's still like summer down here," Morgan commented as the three of them passed the food back and forth between them.

The grass was green and thick. Flowering vines and shrubs filled the patio with sweet fragrance. Two palm trees swayed gently in the balmy breeze, hinting that the night would be a tropical paradise. Yet Lauren knew that more often than not there was trouble in paradise.

"Was it cold in Mena when you left this morning?"

Lauren nodded. "Cold but clear. All the leaves have fallen now. It's looking like turkey time."

Hattie glanced at Morgan. "I hear you're in the milling business. What kind of lumber do you cut?"

"All kinds. Pine and hardwood," he answered.

"I've been to Mena before. Several years ago. It's

beautiful there.'' Hattie stopped and wrinkled her nose. ''But I'm a warm-weather bird.''

''Morgan called me a snowbird,'' Lauren said with a smile, ''because I found it so cold back home.''

Lauren felt him look at her, and warmth tinged her cheeks. That had happened the night he'd taken her out to dinner. He hadn't been indifferent to her then. He'd held her hand across the dinner table, and when they'd sat alone in the car he'd kissed her passionately. But that was in the past, she thought, and better forgotten.

When the meal was over, Lauren tried her best to help her aunt clear the mess away, but Hattie wouldn't hear of it.

''You and Morgan go see if there's anything else that needs to be packed. I'll have this cleared away in no time.''

Lauren knew it would be useless to argue with her aunt. Instead, she rose from the redwood picnic table and headed toward the house. When she pulled back the screen door to enter the kitchen, she was surprised to see Morgan there behind her.

He followed her into the house and down the narrow hallway leading to the room she and Scott had shared.

It was bare now except for the bed and the chest of drawers. Scott's small bed had been removed, and in its place was a stack of boxes holding Lauren's few belongings.

''Is this all?'' Morgan said, looking at the four pasteboard boxes and the one wooden crate.

Lauren crossed to the closet to see if anything had been left hanging. Nothing was there, nor was there anything in the chest. "It looks like it."

"This is all you and Scott have?" he asked, as if the idea of all their belongings fitting into four boxes was incredible to him.

"Yes," she said. "Except for my car, back in Mena. I had some money in savings. But I've already had it transferred to your account. I hope that's all right with you."

His eyes widened even more. "You had your money put in my account?"

Her heart suddenly thumped at the strange look on his face. Obviously, she'd angered him. "Well, we're married now. I thought that's where it belonged."

"Why didn't you ask me first?" he demanded.

"I—I'm sorry, Morgan. If you're worried about my drawing checks on it, there's no need." She gave him a shaky smile, trying her best to make light of it. "I don't have a checkbook, and even if I did, my name is not on the account. I wouldn't draw on your money, anyway."

Morgan felt his jaw clench with pain as he looked at her. He couldn't believe she'd done such a thing. He knew she'd worked hard for what she'd made. And now she was virtually handing it over to him.

"Why did you do it?"

"Because you're taking care of Scott's needs now, and that's what that money was for."

"What about you?"

She brushed his words away with a soft laugh, but

he could hear the tremor in it. "I don't have any needs to speak of."

Wanting desperately to change the subject, Lauren dropped to her knees and lifted the bedspread. "I'll bet Hattie didn't think to look under here," she said. There were two shoe boxes near the head of the bed. Lauren opened the first box to find an old pair of thick-soled work shoes that she'd worn at the salon. There wasn't any need to keep them, so she tossed them in the wastebasket by the bed. The second pair was a worn pair of red tennis shoes. "Well, this one has a little hole, but they'd make good fishing shoes," she said with a wry twist to her mouth. "I know you probably won't ever have time to go fishing, but Scott and I could walk down to the pond behind your house."

Morgan felt a fist inside his chest, twisting his heart tighter and tighter. "Throw the shoes away, Lauren," he said.

She jerked her head up to look at him. He still stood over her. "What?"

"I said throw the shoes away. They're worn out."

"But, Morgan—"

"I won't have a wife of mine wearing worn-out shoes!" he snapped.

Lauren quickly dropped her head, trying to bite back the sting of tears. Slowly she tossed the box into the basket along with the old work shoes. "You might as well face it, Morgan," she whispered hoarsely. "You married a hillbilly. I'm sorry if that embarrasses you."

He didn't say anything. Lauren braced herself and looked up at him. His face was hard with what she could only interpret as anger.

She bit down hard on her bottom lip and jabbed a finger in the direction of the boxes. "Maybe you'd better go through our clothes, Morgan. Because there aren't many things of Scott's or mine that aren't well-worn."

He shook his head, looking in the direction her finger was pointed. "Don't be silly, Lauren."

"I'm not, Morgan," she said, rising to her feet. Quickly she moved over to the boxes and broke the masking tape holding down the four flaps. "Why, by the time we go through these things you'll probably decide this whole trip was for nothing."

"Lauren—" he said in a warning voice.

"These are Scott's play jeans, and I know the knees are worn white, but you'll soon learn that little boys have a habit of playing on their knees," she went on, deliberately ignoring his threatening look. "But he does have a good pair that we save for special occasions like going with me to the grocery store."

She dug deeper in the box and pulled out a cream-colored blouse with a hand-crocheted collar. "Now, this might stand up to Sinclair standards. I paid far more for it than I should have, but I only wear it on rare occasions, so as not to ruin it." She looked at him and laughed shakily. "I even wore this on a date. Can you believe that some man down here in the big city wanted to date a backwoods thing like me? But don't worry, Morgan. Your memory did you proud. It never failed to remind me that no man can be trusted. So the next time he asked I said no.''

Morgan snatched the blouse from her hand and pushed it back in the box. ''That's enough, Lauren.''

''But we've only looked at two things,'' she said.

Morgan knew she was close to crying. He could hear it in her voice, could see it in the trembling of her fingers. He wanted more than anything to pull her into his arms and tell her he didn't want her to hurt, didn't want her to cry. To tell her he didn't want her to hate him for all that had happened to tear them apart.

But there was such a chasm between them now that he feared it could never be crossed unless she met him halfway. Morgan had learned a lot about pride these past few days. His pride wouldn't let him see past the wrong she'd done to him, and he was beginning to see that Lauren had an abundance of pride, too.

''I didn't mean to offend you about the shoes, Lauren,'' he said, his voice softening.

The unexpected statement brought a tearful lump to her throat. For a moment she pressed her palms against her eyes and did her best to collect herself.

''You're right, Morgan,'' she said after a moment. ''I shouldn't be so defensive.''

He made a frustrated sound, then said, ''I just—I want you and Scott to have whatever you need. You don't have to worry about stretching money now.''

Lauren looked at him, wondering if he really

thought that was all she and Scott needed from him. Just his Sinclair money? She suddenly realized that her heart wasn't gone after all. It still had that basic need for him and his love, and not the things his money could buy. Couldn't he see that? Wasn't it written all over her?

With a sort of fatalistic resignation, she began to fasten the flaps down on the box. "Well, maybe we'd better load these things into the truck," she suggested tiredly. "It's getting late, and I expect you'll want to get an early start in the morning."

Before Morgan could reply, Hattie's face appeared around the door. "Does it look like I've packed everything?"

Lauren nodded. "I think so. What about Scott's toys?"

Hattie came into the room and pointed to the wooden crate. "They're in the crate." She glanced at Morgan and laughed. "If it looks like Lauren doesn't have many things, put it down to the fact that she's as tight as bark on a tree—and stubborn, too. Wouldn't let me and Bob buy her a thing. I hope she'll let you spoil her and Scott. They deserve it."

Smiling faintly, Morgan told her, "I'm sure Lauren's worked hard. But don't worry about her now. I'll see that she and Scott are well cared for."

Lauren was glad to see that Morgan wasn't showing Hattie any of the coldness he'd shown her. It would be nice to think Hattie believed that they were a loving couple and that Morgan hadn't married her only for Scott's sake.

Hattie patted Morgan on the arm. "Of course you will. I won't worry about her at all. But I will miss her," she said, casting Lauren a sad little smile. Then, looking back at Morgan, she said, "To be honest, when Lauren first told me that she wanted to go back to Mena and tell you about Scott, I was very skeptical. I didn't want her to go."

Lauren's gaze flashed to Morgan's face. Would he still think she was lying now?

Morgan's eyes darted to Lauren. Could it be that she'd been telling the truth? he wondered desperately. Had she really come home to tell him about Scott?

"Why was that?" he asked, forcing his attention back to Hattie.

"Oh, I thought you might turn out to be one of those men who wouldn't care about Lauren or Scott. But now—" she beamed happily at them both, making Lauren feel like a complete fraud and Morgan like a two-inch heel "—well, now I can see how much you care for Lauren, and it makes me happy that you're married and together now."

Unable to take any more, Lauren reached for one of the boxes. "We'd better get these loaded, Aunt Hattie. I still have to call Juanita tonight and arrange for her to deal with my things at the salon."

Lauren scooted quickly out the door, thinking that if she heard another word about loving and caring she'd burst into tears and confess the whole miserable mess to her aunt.

By eleven that night, Lauren and Morgan had everything loaded into the truck and she'd taken care of her business with the salon.

Hattie had talked herself nearly hoarse and was now yawning delicately. "It's really selfish of me to keep you two up when you have to get up early in the morning," she told them, rising from her arm-chair. "So I'm going to say good-night and let you go to bed."

Lauren's eyes widened on her aunt's back. *Go to bed!* My Lord, there were only two beds in the house. That meant she and Morgan would have to share the same bed!

"Er, uh... Aunt Hattie?"

"Yes, dear?" she asked, glancing at Lauren.

Lauren darted a wild look at Morgan, then jerked her eyes back to Hattie. She couldn't say anything about the sleeping arrangements without spilling the truth. It would seem strange indeed to tell her aunt that she and Morgan needed separate beds.

"I—I just wanted to say good-night, and thanks for your help."

Hattie gave her a sleepy smile, yawning again. "Good night, darling. I'll see you in the morning."

Once Hattie was out of sight, Morgan unwound his long frame from the couch, stood and stretched with masculine grace. Lauren's eyes followed his move-ments with a sense of panic.

"I think Hattie's right about us turning in. We've got a long day ahead of us," he said.

Lauren swallowed and pushed herself to her feet. "You're ready to go to bed?" she blurted.

The arch of his brow said he found her question rather inane. "Yes. Why?"

With pleading eyes, Lauren took a step toward him. "Morgan," she whispered, "we have to sleep together."

Chapter Ten

Morgan's eyes narrowed until it was impossible for Lauren to tell what he was thinking.

"We have to sleep together? Is this your idea of a joke?" he hissed under his breath.

Her nostrils flared at the sardonic question. "Do you see me laughing?"

No, she was far from laughing, he thought. In fact, she was visibly trembling, making him wonder if she was frightened or repulsed by the idea of sleeping with him.

"There's only one bed?" he asked.

Lauren nodded ruefully, and Morgan glanced over his shoulder at the short couch. It wouldn't be comfortable, but he could manage.

She followed the direction of his gaze. "Morgan, you can't sleep on the couch."

"Can't?" he questioned dryly. "What is this, Lauren? Are you planning on seducing me?"

Lauren's nerves snapped, and she turned on her heel, muttering, "Morgan, you're the last man on earth I'd want to seduce!"

He caught up to her before she reached the hall. When his hand came down on her shoulder, she twisted around to glare at him.

"Then why do you want me to share your bed?" he asked.

The mockery in his voice was gone, and Lauren felt herself grow limp beneath the heavy weight of his hand. Fastening her eyes on a button of his shirt, she said, "Because...because Aunt Hattie...she thinks you love me. If you sleep on the couch—I don't want her to know that we don't...do that. Well, she'd be hurt and worried about me."

Morgan's chest heaved out a long breath. "I see," he said after a moment. "Then, for appearances, I suppose we can make do for tonight."

With immense relief, Lauren raised her eyes to his. "Thank you, Morgan."

The bedroom seemed smaller than ever when she and Morgan entered and shut the door behind them. Since they'd moved the boxes and all the things that had once belonged to her and Scott were stripped away from the room, it seemed very bare. The starkness matched the feeling in Lauren's heart as she looked at the empty double bed.

"There's only one bathroom, across the hall," she

told Morgan. "If you'd like to go first, I'll turn down the covers."

Morgan left with his traveling bag and Lauren began to fold down the crisp sheet and light blanket. Her hands were a bit unsteady as she finished the task.

How could she possibly relax and go to sleep with Morgan only a few inches away from her? She knew he had no desire to touch her, but that didn't keep her from wanting him.

In only a few minutes, he returned. Lauren gathered up her toiletries and her nightclothes and left the bedroom.

Thank goodness her gown was plain cotton. At least Morgan couldn't accuse her of wearing something meant to attract him, she thought, brushing her hair loose over her shoulders.

Staring at her image in the medicine-chest mirror, she decided that her pale face and hollow eyes would be a turnoff to any man.

When she returned from the bathroom, the light was off and Morgan was already in bed. The faint glow of a streetlamp filtered through the blinds, throwing slatted bars of yellow across the bed.

She could see Morgan lying on his side, his back turned to her. She shed her robe and climbed in beside him, her heart thumping out of control. Lauren couldn't explain her reaction to him. She knew there was virtually no chance of anything happening between them, but still, being with him in such a close, intimate way gave her a strange, smothered feeling.

Lauren lay rigid, as close to the edge of the mattress as possible, and forced her eyes closed. After a few moments she began to breathe more normally.

Lauren could hear the familiar muted sound of traffic in the distance. She had lain in this bedroom for the past four years and thought of Morgan. Now he was here beside her. But they were no closer now than before, when they'd been living hundreds of miles apart.

Suddenly Morgan rolled onto his back. His voice sounded in the darkness.

"Did Scott sleep with you in this room?" he asked.

Lauren kept her back to him. "Yes. He had a small bed of his own."

A few seconds passed. Then he said, "Your aunt is a very nice woman. She reminds me of your mother, in a way. I like her."

Lauren was surprised by his generous comment. It was something the old Morgan would have said, and she warmed to it.

Turning onto her back, too, she said, "Aunt Hattie likes you, too. I can tell."

"What did you tell her all those years ago? About me, I mean?"

Lauren opened her eyes and stared at the dappled shadows moving along the ceiling. "I told her the truth. That you didn't want to marry me."

Morgan could have argued that point, but he found he didn't want to. He was beginning to see that in Lauren's heart she'd taken his words four years ago as an outright rejection. Well, he would take the blame for that. She'd been so young. Too young to understand what he was trying to do for her, for them. In the end, his making love to her had hurt her in ways he'd never foreseen. And no matter what, that fact filled him with deep remorse. Each time he thought of her alone and pregnant with his child, alone and raising their baby, he felt sick and hollow inside.

"Apparently she's forgiven me for that," he said.

Lauren swallowed and closed her eyes. "Yes, I suppose she has."

But I haven't.

Morgan could feel her unspoken words dangling between them. It was the last thought that ran through his mind before he fell asleep.

Lauren woke suddenly, her heart thumping in her chest. Where was she? What was that unfamiliar warmth against her? That weight on her legs?

Turning her head on the pillow, she saw Morgan's face only inches away, and it all came back to her. They'd had to share the bed. But something had happened in the night. She was now snuggled against the hard length of him, and one of his bare legs was thrown possessively over both of hers.

Her breath caught in her throat, and she started to ease carefully out of his grasp.

He groaned and stirred at the movements. Then his hand clamped down on the side of her waist and tugged her back against him.

"Morgan..." she breathed, unsure if he was aware of his hold on her.

His eyes opened to see the pale oval of Lauren's face, the spread of her black hair against the pillow. This time he knew what he was reaching for.

"Don't pull away, Lauren," he whispered. "Come here. To me."

Mesmerized by the longing in his voice, Lauren met his gaze, and her eyes locked with his. Slowly his hand rose and pushed into the tumble of curls lying against her cheek.

She moaned at the tender touch and turned to lean against him.

Her faint movement of surrender was to Morgan like a douse of kerosene on a flame. His hand thrust deeper into her hair and drew her face down to his.

Lauren's senses were spinning madly as his mouth closed over hers in a savage, hungry way. For some reason he wanted her, and she could not deny, even to herself, that she wanted him, too.

Soft sounds came from her throat as his arms moved around her, pulled her so close that her breasts flattened against his chest.

Her hands found his shoulders, and she felt the smoothness of his skin, the hard strength of his muscles. Touching him was like finally giving in to a forbidden addiction. She didn't know what tomorrow would bring, but she knew tonight she would take, without question, what he offered.

Lauren's soft warmth fired an unquenchable desire in Morgan's veins. He had wanted her for so long. Not just the past few weeks, but all through the time she'd been away from him. The time, the missing, the aching, the wanting her, had left him with a hunger so deep that he shook with it.

His tongue thrust deep into the cavern of her mouth, taking the sweetness of it and searching for a needed response.

Lauren did not disappoint him. She wound her arms tightly around his neck and wove her legs through his.

Morgan's hands came to life, caressing and stroking her body in a thousand different places and a thousand different ways. Each touch swept Lauren higher and higher, until she was breathless and panting. The need to become one with him was like a fierce hunger inside her.

The cotton gown became an annoying barrier for both of them. Morgan tugged it over her head and tossed it on the floor.

Then it was flesh against flesh, heart against heart. The scent of her filled Morgan's senses, and he knew this was the same scent that had haunted him these past weeks. This was his wife, the woman he loved. He could no longer resist her.

"Little one," he murmured against her lips. "My little one."

"Oh, Morgan... Morgan..." Lauren gasped, unable to say more. She wanted to say "I love you," but fear stopped the words in her throat. She was afraid to say anything that might break the spell between them.

In one smooth motion Morgan rolled her beneath

him and parted her thighs with his knee. Lauren's low moan was lost beneath his lips as he thrust into her softness.

Their lovemaking was swift, torrid and complete. When it was over she was drained and slow to pull her shattered senses back together.

Their overheated bodies were slick with sweat. As Morgan rolled away from her, the air chilled her moist skin. She turned her head on the pillow to see him lying on his back, his forearm resting across his eyes.

He seemed a long distance away from her, even though they had just made love. Yet she knew that in spite of the physical satisfaction they'd shared there had been something missing between them.

Love, she thought sadly. Nothing had any meaning without it.

Rolling onto her side, she reached out and touched his chest. "Morgan, why did you make love to me?"

Slowly he allowed his arm to fall away, and his brown eyes met hers. In the glow of the streetlamp Lauren could see them traveling over her face, as if he were searching for an answer, an answer that should have come easily.

"Because you're my wife," he said finally.

It was not what she needed or wanted to hear. But then, Lauren supposed, to expect more would be foolish on her part. At least he hadn't lied and pretended it had been for love.

An ache crept into her breast, and she turned away

from him in fear that tears would fall and he would see them.

Moments later she felt Morgan's arm come around her waist. Without a word he pulled her against him. Lauren rested her head against his shoulder and stared dry-eyed into the darkness.

It was well after dark when Lauren and Morgan arrived back in Mena. They drove by Eileen's first to pick up Scott. The boy had fallen asleep on his grandmother's couch, but he awoke bright-eyed and ready to chatter when he saw that his parents had arrived.

"It's good to be home," Lauren said when Morgan pulled into the drive of their own house.

Morgan glanced across the seat at his wife. Scott clutched her tightly around the neck, unwilling as yet to let his mother get even a few inches away from him.

"It's cold and dead-looking compared to Houston," he said, surprised but pleased that Lauren now considered his home her home, too.

"I'll trade palms for pines any day," she told him. "Mena has always been home to me."

Lauren went ahead with Scott to unlock the door while Morgan hoisted a couple of the boxes out of the bed of the pickup. The wind was blowing strong and cold from the north, whistling through the pines in the backyard. Scott shivered, waiting for Lauren to maneuver the key in the lock.

Morgan was right behind them when she pushed the door open and clicked on the lights. The house felt blessedly warm. Lauren looked around at the now-familiar furnishings and felt as if she had crossed a threshold in her life. Her and Scott's life in Houston was gone now. The sight of Morgan carrying in their things seemed to finalize that.

While Morgan finished bringing in the remaining boxes, Lauren went to the kitchen to prepare sandwiches and hot chocolate.

In order to make the trip faster, they'd only eaten a light snack in the truck while they'd traveled, and that had been several hours ago. Lauren was hungry, and she knew that Morgan, always a big eater, had to be starving.

She had the ham-and-cheese and turkey sandwiches on the table by the time Morgan appeared in the kitchen.

"Everything is in the house. I opened the crate of toys for Scott. He's in there now, digging into them."

Lauren smiled faintly. "Maybe some of the old toys he'd grown tired of will look interesting to him now."

Morgan joined her at the table and picked up one of the turkey sandwiches. Lauren began to eat, also, wondering all the while if things would be different now that they were home, now that they'd made love.

From the way Morgan was acting, Lauren doubted it. Since they'd awaken early this morning and left Houston, he'd behaved as if nothing had happened between them. There had been no soft looks, no sweet words, no mention of love or wanting or needing.

That had left Lauren wounded and wondering where their marriage was headed.

Morgan ate two sandwiches, and Lauren got up to refill his cup of chocolate. He reached into his back pocket and pulled out his billfold. She watched with faint curiosity as he slipped out some cards.

"Here are three major credit cards. I want you to take them tomorrow and get whatever you and Scott need," he told her.

Stunned, she eased back slowly in her chair. "Morgan, that isn't necessary. We have—"

He gave her a look that brooked no argument. "It's wintertime now, and it will be cold for several months to come. Scott needs to be dressed properly, and so do you."

Morgan pushed the cards across the table at Lauren. She stared at them as if they represented vipers instead of money.

"Morgan, I wouldn't feel right—"

He grimaced and jammed the billfold back in his jeans. "Why? Don't you feel like my wife?"

She blushed at the question, thinking of how he'd made her his wife in the physical sense. But that wasn't enough for Lauren. She knew that love hadn't been his motive, and without love there was no sense of sharing or rightness about anything. "I just— It's your money. I don't feel right about using it just because we signed a marriage license."

Morgan had thought he could marry Lauren and remain indifferent to her. What a mistake that had been! And now it hurt him to know that she didn't think of herself as his wife, his equal. Common sense told him that was his fault. But Lauren had injured his pride and broken his trust in her, he reasoned with himself. He wanted to tell her he loved her. But he didn't know if he could trust her with his love again. He wasn't even sure Lauren would believe him now.

"We signed that marriage license for Scott's sake," he said dryly. "Maybe you can force yourself to use my money for the same reason."

His words stung like a slap. Without looking at him, she swept up the cards and jammed them into her purse which was lying on top of the refrigerator. "I'll buy whatever I think necessary," she told him.

Once Lauren had cleared away the mess in the kitchen, she went into the living room and played with Scott on the floor.

From an armchair, Morgan pretended to watch the news on the television, but actually he was watching his wife and son. They'd been playing a game with toy cars, but now Lauren had him pinned in a playful wrestling match. He was glad to see that Lauren did not mollycoddle Scott, as some mothers did their sons. She played rough, the way little boys liked. Scott's loud squeals and giggles made it hard to hear the news commentator's voice, but Morgan didn't mind. Seeing Lauren and Scott happy together made him feel contented in a way he never had been before.

After a while, Lauren took Scott to the bathroom for a wash. She changed him into his pajamas, then sent him back out to the living room while she gathered her lingerie and toiletries for a bath.

Lauren was lying in a tub of hot water and bubbles when the door creaked open behind her. "Scott," she said in a scolding tone, "you should be asleep by now. Not here in—"

Morgan's voice interrupted her. "Scott is asleep."

Lauren jerked her head around in shock. "Morgan, I thought—"

He moved into the bathroom. "I put Scott to bed. He fell asleep on the couch."

"Oh, I would have been out in a few minutes to get him."

His face was deceptively expressionless, but his brown eyes were gleaming as they took in her wet breasts and shoulders, then moved farther down to where the water lapped against her waist.

"Scott is my son. I want to care for him, too."

Morgan did love Scott. That much she could easily see. She just wished his love could include her.

"Yes, of course you do," she murmured. Then she had to gulp for breath when he squatted on his heels beside the tub.

One corner of Morgan's mouth lifted, as though he didn't mind her knowing that he liked looking at her all shiny and wet and naked.

His gaze, in turn, was arousing her and washing her in a sensual wave of heat. Lauren wondered if he knew what he was doing to her.

Wordlessly he took the bar of soap from her hand and rubbed it slowly between his palms. Lauren swallowed and closed her eyes when his strong hands slid across the mounds of her breasts. His skin was work-worn, and the abrasiveness of it, coupled with the slick soap, make his caresses highly erotic.

By the time his hand lowered beneath the water and slipped between her thighs, she was totally lost in him. Her head fell limply back against his arm, and instantly she felt his lips come upon hers.

She wanted him shamelessly and that fact made her heart ache. He didn't love her. He only wanted her body. But she couldn't fight the languid pleasure his touch gave her. She couldn't fight the love she felt for him.

Their kiss was hot and greedy. Before it ended, Morgan's right arm had slid beneath her knees. She clung to his neck as he lifted her from the water and carried her through the doorway to the bedroom.

Mindless of her wet body, Morgan deposited her on the wide bed and quickly went about shedding his boots and jeans.

Lauren watched him in the darkness. His body was a magnificent thing, tall and heavily muscled, his shoulders broad, his waist lean. She hungered for it as the memory of last night's passion awakened her senses to the pleasures ahead.

When Morgan joined her on the bed and took her into his arms, Lauren sighed soulfully. He framed her face with his hands and kissed her softly, first her upper lip, then the lower.

This was his wife, and he needed to know that somewhere inside her was the same girl he'd fallen in love with all those years ago. He wanted, needed desperately, for that Lauren to be in his life, in his heart. He wanted to see love sparkle in her eyes, to see her smile at him as she used to do. He wanted to love her, to take away the hurt he'd caused her. He was determined to get the old Lauren back, no matter how long it took, no matter how slowly he had to go about doing it.

Chapter Eleven

The bell over the salon door tinkled as Lauren allowed the plate glass to close behind her.

Gypsy was on the telephone. While Lauren waited for her friend to end her conversation, she shed her coat and hung it on a rack in a corner of the room.

It was early morning, and the shop was empty. Lauren sat down in a padded chair and ran a hand over her damp hair.

Rain had been falling for the past hour, and the weather forecast had said snow would be here by nightfall.

"Hello, beautiful," Gypsy said cheerfully after she'd hung up the receiver and written down an appointment. "Are you ready for a new hairdo?"

Lauren smiled halfheartedly. "I suppose. Though I don't know why. It's going to get wet anyway."

Gypsy laughed, dismissing Lauren's downcast mood. "You sound like me telling Mom there's no use washing the dishes 'cause they're only going to get dirty again."

Lauren smiled wryly and followed Gypsy over to the main work area. On the way there, Gypsy glanced between the slatted blinds. "Mmm, yes, it is still raining, isn't it? Maybe it will turn to snow."

"I wouldn't mind that. It's been a long time since I've seen snow."

"Hey, look at that new Mustang. Boy, would I love to have one like that! A cherry-red convertible. Wonder how many perms I'd have to give a year to make the payments," Gypsy said wistfully.

"Too many, Gypsy."

"You say that like you know."

"I do. The car is mine."

Gypsy's eyes widened, and then she laughed. "You're kidding!"

Settling down in the work chair, Lauren shook her head. "No. Morgan traded in my little economy car and bought the Mustang for me."

Gypsy laughed incredulously. "What a darling he must be! Were you surprised?"

Gypsy whipped a plastic cape around Lauren's neck and fastened it tightly.

Lauren sighed. "Overwhelmed is more like it."

Lauren's friend gave her a strange look. "Why do you say that? Don't you like it?"

Lauren avoided Gypsy's gaze. "The car is very nice. I'd be crazy not to like it. But—"

Gypsy looked at her impatiently. "But what? What could possibly be bad about your husband getting you a new car? Unless, of course, he couldn't afford it and had to sell the family china."

Lauren lifted her hand, then let it fall helplessly back against the chair. "Morgan can more than afford the car," she explained. "It's just that...I think he did it because he was embarrassed by my old car. It was a disgrace to him for me to drive it around."

"God, Lauren, you're more messed up than I first believed," Gypsy groaned.

She flipped a knob on the chair and pushed Lauren's head back in the shampoo bowl.

Lauren looked miserably up at her old friend. "You don't understand, Gypsy. I feel like—" How could she tell Gypsy how she felt? Lauren didn't even know how she was feeling anymore.

Since the night they'd returned from Houston—almost a month ago—Lauren had moved her things into Morgan's bedroom. It had been an unspoken concession between them. Morgan didn't hide the fact that he wanted her physically, and Lauren couldn't hide her desire for him. It would have been futile to even try.

So now she woke beside him, slept beside him, cooked his meals, cleaned his house and cared for their son. She was his wife in every sense—almost. The only thing missing was love, and that missing ingredient was leaving Lauren dispirited. She wondered how she could possibly live out the rest of her life yearning for something she couldn't have.

She took a deep breath and tried to explain it all to Gypsy. "I feel like nothing has changed. I think that four years ago Morgan didn't want to marry me because—because I wasn't good enough to be his wife. And now—well, because of Scott, his sense of duty forced him to marry me. And he's trying to gloss me over, I guess. He made me buy a whole new wardrobe for myself and Scott. He's given me credit cards, a checkbook and a checking account with a balance big enough to choke a horse. Then this car— Oh, Gypsy, I— Why can't he just love me? Love me just for me, just for the country girl I've always been?"

Gypsy heard the misery in Lauren's voice and smiled with gentle reassurance, smoothing her hand over her friend's furrowed brow.

"Have you ever stopped to think that he's doing all of this because he *does* love you?"

Lauren shook her head. "If Morgan ever loved me, I managed to kill that by keeping Scott a secret."

"There is such a thing as forgiveness, you know." Gypsy adjusted the water, then turned the spray on Lauren's scalp. "Love can survive most anything if it's strong enough. And speaking of forgiveness, you could stand to do a little of that yourself."

Confused, Lauren looked up at Gypsy. "What do you mean?"

"I mean that you need to quit dwelling on the past.

Forgive him for hurting you. If you can't, how do you expect Morgan to ever forgive you?''

She began to massage shampoo into Lauren's hair. The soothing sensation made Lauren close her eyes and think about her friend's words.

Lauren knew Gypsy was right. Forgiving was a part of loving. Could she find it in her heart to forgive Morgan?

Yes. She wanted to forget all that past hurt. Put it behind them both. She wanted Morgan to forgive her for keeping their son a secret, for not understanding his needs and wants. But how could she let him know? Would he even want to hear it?

In this past month, much of his coldness toward her had disappeared, but she knew he was a long way from loving her. He wanted her for a bed partner, and he wanted her to mother his son. Somehow she had to make him want her as a wife in the true sense of the word. She had to make him see that they could be truly happy together if he could love her even half as much as she loved him.

Gypsy trimmed Lauren's hair, then blow-dried it. Afterward, the two women shared a cup of coffee.

''It's only a week until Christmas,'' Lauren said, buttoning herself into her coat. ''I'd love for you to come out and help us celebrate. Why don't you drive out and have supper next Friday night? I've already made all kinds of fudge and cookies.''

Gypsy's slim face brightened. ''I'd love to come. May I bring a date, too?''

Lauren chuckled. "Of course. Who is he?"

Gypsy shrugged and got to her feet. "I don't know yet. But I'll find him by then. You don't think Morgan will mind?"

Lauren started toward the door. "Don't be silly. Morgan has always liked you. He says you're like a peacock in a barnyard of chickens."

Gypsy laughed. "Did he really? I'll have to thank him for that. And Lauren..." she added as her friend started out the door, "Morgan loves you. You just haven't realized it yet."

Lauren smiled, albeit doubtfully. "I'd give the world for you to be right, Gypsy."

By the time Morgan came home from the mill that night, it was snowing.

Scott, who'd had his nose pressed against the window as he'd watched for his father, squealed happily at Morgan's arrival. Before Lauren could stop him, the child ran through the door and scrambled down the walk.

She watched misty-eyed as Morgan lifted the boy up onto his shoulders. He hesitated long enough to point out the trees and different objects that were now becoming snow-covered. By the time her son and husband entered the house, white flakes were clinging to their clothes and hair.

Scott cried excitedly, "Mama, the ground is white and Goldy has snow all over her hair!"

Lauren laughed. "And so do you. Can you shake your head like Goldy does?"

Morgan set Scott on his feet. The young boy promptly attempted an imitation of the gold Labrador.

Morgan looked at Lauren. She sat on the couch, her feet curled beneath her, wearing jeans and a red sweater. The bright color looked beautiful next to her black hair and her cherry-colored lips. But she was very pale and, not for the first time, Morgan felt a pang of worry. She'd seemed very lethargic over the past couple of weeks. He didn't know if something was wrong with her health or if she found living with him so depressing that it was affecting her physically.

"Hello, Lauren," he said, unzipping his coat.

She uncurled herself from the couch and she smiled at him. Morgan's heart swelled. He needed to see her smile so badly, but her lips had rarely curved these past days, unless she'd smiled at their son.

"It's very cold out," she said. "I started to call to see if you needed me to bring your coveralls over to the mill."

"I was in the office most of the afternoon," he told her, secretly elated at her concern. "I finished signing the contract with that logging company I was telling you about."

"That's good news," she said, and took his coat to hang it in the closet. "I've got fried ham and candied sweet potatoes for supper. It's all ready, if you want to go wash."

"Come on, Scott," Morgan told the boy, "I'll beat you to the table."

The child trotted down the hall after his father, and Lauren went into the kitchen.

"You did something to your hair," Morgan said a few minutes later as the three of them sat eating.

Lauren reached up and touched her black curls. She hadn't expected Morgan to notice such a minor thing as a trim. "Yes. Gypsy trimmed it for me. I didn't want to look ragged for the holidays, especially since your sister is coming home."

"It looks very nice."

His words stunned her. Her eyes flew to his face, and she felt her cheeks burning with unaccustomed warmth. "Thank you, Morgan."

"Santa Claus will be here in six days, Daddy. Did you know that?" Scott asked as he crammed sugared potatoes into his little mouth.

Morgan smiled. "I sure did. Have you been good so you'll get lots of toys?"

Scott nodded. "So has Mama. What do you think she'll get from Santa?"

Morgan turned and arched a brow at Lauren. "What does Mama want?" he asked gently.

Morgan made the word sound like an endearment. Her heart lifted, and she smiled broadly at him. "Whatever Santa wants to give me, I suppose."

He laughed softly at that and finished off the last of his coffee. Lauren started to refill his cup, but Morgan shook his head. "That's all I want right now. I have a surprise to bring in."

"A surprise?" Scott echoed.

"Finish your plate and I'll show you," Morgan told him.

A few minutes later Lauren sat on the couch while an excited Scott wiggled in her lap, waiting for Morgan to come through the door.

When he finally appeared, he was dragging a huge blue spruce.

"Oh, Morgan, it's beautiful," Lauren said, suddenly overwhelmed by emotion. She would never have expected him to show such an interest in the holidays or to want to make them nice for her and Scott.

Scott jumped from her lap, shouting, "A Christmas tree! A Christmas tree!"

Morgan got a big box of decorations from the garage, and for the next hour the three of them trimmed the tree.

Since Scott was too small to remember much about last Christmas, he was taking in everything about this one with an excitement he could hardly contain. He chattered nonstop. Morgan answered most of his questions, while Lauren was content to concentrate on hanging the shiny balls on the spruce's thick branches. This was the happiest she'd been since she'd returned to Mena. Gypsy's words turned over once again in her mind.

Morgan loves you. You just haven't realized it yet.

Could Gypsy be right? Her heart ached for it to be so.

"It's truly a beautiful tree, Morgan," Lauren said, standing back to admire their handiwork. "Thank you so much for getting it."

Morgan finished hanging one last ornament before turning to look at her. "This is our first Christmas together. I want it to be special—for all of us," he said gently.

The tenderness in his voice caused tears to form at the backs of her eyes. "So do I," she whispered, not daring to let herself say more. But she did dare to let hope creep into her heart, and it twinkled in her eyes.

Morgan saw it and marveled at it. The spruce had made her much happier than the new car, the clothes or the checking account. He wondered how long it would take him to understand his wife.

"Where does this go, Mama?"

Lauren looked down to see Scott holding a big gold star. "It goes on the very top, and since this tree is so tall, we'll have to let Daddy put it on," she told him.

While Morgan attached the star, Lauren stepped back a few feet to survey the job. "It needs to go a little to the right," she told him.

He turned it a fraction and asked, "How's that?"

"It's— Morgan, I—"

Hearing the strange catch in her voice, Morgan turned around to see Lauren's knees buckling and her hand reaching frantically for something to grasp a hold of.

Somehow he managed to catch her before she fell. Quickly he laid her on the couch, got a wet cloth and washed her face.

"Lauren! Honey, can you hear me?"

Slowly her head turned on the cushion. Then she moaned faintly and her eyes fluttered open. "Morgan…what happened? I was—"

"You fainted," he said gravely. "How do you feel now?"

Lauren pushed at the hair falling in her eyes and attempted to sit up. Morgan stopped her with two big hands on her shoulders.

"Just lie still a minute," he commanded.

"I feel all right," she insisted, but her voice still sounded weak.

He shook his head. "I want you to go to the doctor."

"Morgan," she protested, "it was just a little fainting spell."

His eyes caught and held hers. "Don't argue. I want you to go."

She heard the concern in his voice, and her heart thumped with renewed vigor. If he really cared, she would do it. "I'll go tomorrow," she promised. "Now please let me help finish the tree."

Lauren let herself into the house. In a daze, she removed her coat and hung it in the closet.

She'd just driven home from seeing her old family doctor. He'd worn a broad smile when she'd left the office. Lauren was pregnant. Pregnant with Morgan's second child. The news had shocked her, though now that she'd had some time to think about it she shouldn't have been surprised. These past couple of weeks she'd been tired and had had little appetite.

Morgan had been forced into marrying her because of Scott. Would he think she'd deliberately let herself get pregnant to get a tighter hold on him? He loved Scott, but that didn't mean he wanted another child with her, or so soon.

Last night everything had seemed so much better. She had even let herself believe that things could be worked out between them. But now...now she didn't know about anything.

Suddenly she dropped down onto the couch and burst into sobs. Already she loved and wanted this baby. How could she not, when she loved Morgan so much? But since Morgan didn't return that love, there was a good chance he wouldn't be happy about the news. It would drive yet another wedge between them.

The telephone sounded in the quiet house to cut into Lauren's misery. She wiped her eyes and did her best to sniff back her tears.

"Hello."

"Lauren, did you make it back from the doctor's office?"

It was Morgan. Her hands began to tremble. "Yes."

"What did he say?"

"I— I'm—I'm all right," she said in a jerky voice.

"Lauren! You're crying. What's the matter?" he asked, his voice growing brusque and serious.

"Nothing. He—he assured me I was fine," she finally managed to say. And it was the truth. Dr. Gates had said she was as healthy as a horse.

"You sure as hell don't sound fine," he barked.

"Morgan—"

"I'm coming home."

She stared at the receiver for a long time after it went dead.

When Morgan let himself into the house he found Lauren sitting in a rocker in the bedroom watching the snow fall, joining what had already frosted the pine trees in the backyard.

Morgan stopped for a moment in the doorway, taking in her forlorn expression. He knew at that moment that Lauren was his life. Without her there would be no light or joy. He knew that she was the reason he had lived alone in this house for the past four years. He'd been waiting. Waiting for her to come home to him. Now he couldn't bear to think of losing her.

She must have sensed his presence, because she turned away from the window to look at him.

"You shouldn't have bothered to come home," she said in a flat voice. "I told you I was all right."

He moved into the room. When he reached her he

squatted beside the rocker and took her face between his palms. Tears still scarred her face.

"Something is wrong. Are you seriously ill and just not telling me?"

"No."

He let out a relieved breath. "Then what is it? Have you decided you can no longer bear to live with me? That you want a divorce?"

Lauren stared at him in amazement. Was that what he thought? That she wanted to leave him? Oh, God! "No, that is not what I want!"

His thumb reached out to wipe away a tear that fell from her green eyes. "Then why are you crying?"

"Because—because I'm pregnant," she whispered in a shaken voice.

The color drained away from his tanned face to leave it a sickly, sallow hue. "You don't want it? You don't want to have my baby?"

The question was ripped from him, as though to ask it was as painful to him as the idea that she did not want to bear him another child.

Lauren reared back at the impact of his question. How could he think she would not want his child? *Their* child? Couldn't he feel it every time they made love? "Of course I want it, Morgan!"

His eyes searched her face. "You don't look like you do."

"That's because—because I thought you wouldn't want it. That you'd accuse me of trying to trap you further in this marriage."

Joy, like sweet wine, poured over him. He reached out for her, pulled her out of the chair and into his arms. "My darling, my little darling, haven't you figured out by now that I *want* to be trapped? That our marriage means more to me than anything?"

Her head shook against his shoulder. "You only married me because of Scott."

"I was planning to ask you to marry me even before I discovered Scott was my child."

Lauren pulled her head back just enough to see his face. "But you said—"

"I said lots of things because I was hurt and angry at what you'd done," he told her.

"I deserved your anger, Morgan. No matter what, I should have never kept Scott from you," she said sorrowfully. "Can you ever forgive me?"

His eyes softened. "Can you forgive me for hurting you all those years ago? For not being there when Scott was born?"

Happiness surged up inside Lauren like a great wave that could not be contained. Love, pure and simple, was in his face.

"Yes!" she cried happily. "I already have. None of that matters anymore, Morgan. I just want to hear you say that you want our baby."

He groaned and cradled her head against his chest, cherishing the feel of her in his arms. "How could I not want it? I love you, Lauren. I suppose I've never stopped loving you."

"I never stopped loving you," she confessed. "But why didn't you tell me? These past weeks—"

"I'd said and done so many terrible things to you that I was afraid you wouldn't believe me. I thought it would be better to try to show you." Suddenly he laughed with great pleasure and spanned his hand across her flat tummy.

"Obviously I got carried away with showing you."

Her hands came up to frame his face, and she kissed him, slowly and lingeringly. "I was so miserable thinking you didn't love me. That you only wanted me physically."

"Oh, Lauren," he protested. "How could you think—"

"When I was nineteen, I believed you turned away from me because you saw me as a little hillbilly. Good enough for sex, but not good enough to be your wife. It did something to me, Morgan. I was always so proud of who I was, what I was, until we parted. Then I had to take a second look, and that look was painful. Now, since we've married— Well, the clothes, the car— I couldn't help thinking you were still ashamed of me."

"Oh, God, Lauren," he said, his face twisted with anguish, "I guess I've done everything wrong. The more I tried to show you how much I love you, the more I seemed to make a mess of things. But believe me when I tell you I've never, never been ashamed of you. You're the woman I love. And that hillbilly heart of yours, as you call it, is the part I love the most."

"Oh, Morgan, I love you so very much," Lauren whispered, happy tears sparkling in her eyes.

He kissed her over and over until she was breathless and laughing.

Laughing along with her, he pulled her to her feet and started out of the bedroom.

"Where are we going?" she asked curiously.

"Down to tell Scott that he has a new baby brother or sister on the way."

In the living room, they pulled on their coats. While Lauren buttoned hers she admired the blue spruce with all its bright decorations. Christmas was truly on its way.

She tossed Morgan a coy grin and said, "Now I already know what Santa's giving me for being good."

His lips curling into a sexy smile, he reached for her and pressed her bundled form against his. "My pleasure, Mrs. Sinclair," he murmured and planted a lingering kiss on her lips. "Would it be okay if he gave you the same thing next Christmas?"

"Morgan!" she said with throaty laughter. "How many children do you want?"

He chuckled and traced his forefinger across her cheekbone. "Oh, I don't know. We'll start counting after the third or fourth."

"There are only two bedrooms in this house. Where will we put them all?" she asked.

Morgan looked at her with joy and amusement. "Are you forgetting I own a lumber mill? We'll build a two-story if necessary."

Her arms hugged his lean waist. "We're going to be very happy, darling," she whispered. "I'm going to spend the rest of my life loving you, making up for the time we lost."

"There'll be no more lost time," he assured her with a kiss.

Out on the porch they watched the wind blow the fat white flakes horizontally. Morgan reached for Lauren and swept her up in his arms.

"I don't want you to fall in the snow," he told her as she squealed in surprise.

Laughing, Lauren hugged him and pressed her cheek against his as he started out across the yard and down to the main house. She'd been so terribly alone while bearing Scott, but now she had never felt so loved and pampered.

"Morgan, there's nothing wrong with me, you know. I'm perfectly capable of walking."

"So you are," he murmured tenderly. But he carried her the whole distance just the same.

*   *   *   *   *

American HEROES
AGAINST ALL ODDS

1. ALABAMA
After Hours—Gina Wilkins

2. ALASKA
The Bride Came C.O.D.—Barbara Bretton

3. ARIZONA
Stolen Memories—Kelsey Roberts

4. ARKANSAS
Hillbilly Heart—Stella Bagwell

5. CALIFORNIA
Stevie's Chase—Justine Davis

6. COLORADO
Walk Away, Joe—Pamela Toth

7. CONNECTICUT
Honeymoon for Hire—Cathy Gillen Thacker

8. DELAWARE
Death Spiral—Patricia Rosemoor

9. FLORIDA
Cry Uncle—Judith Arnold

10. GEORGIA
Safe Haven—Marilyn Pappano

11. HAWAII
Marriage Incorporated—Debbi Rawlins

12. IDAHO
Plain Jane's Man—Kristine Rolofson

13. ILLINOIS
Safety of His Arms—Vivian Leiber

14. INDIANA
A Fine Spring Rain—Celeste Hamilton

15. IOWA
Exclusively Yours—Leigh Michaels

16. KANSAS
The Doubletree—Victoria Pade

17. KENTUCKY
Run for the Roses—Peggy Moreland

18. LOUISIANA
Rambler's Rest—Bay Matthews

19. MAINE
Whispers in the Wood—Helen R. Myers

20. MARYLAND
Chance at a Lifetime—Anne Marie Winston

21. MASSACHUSETTS
Body Heat—Elise Title

22. MICHIGAN
Devil's Night—Jennifer Greene

23. MINNESOTA
Man from the North Country—Laurie Paige

24. MISSISSIPPI
Miss Charlotte Surrenders—Cathy Gillen Thacker

25. MISSOURI
One of the Good Guys—Carla Cassidy

26. MONTANA
Angel—Ruth Langan

27. NEBRASKA
Return to Raindance—Phyllis Halldorson

28. NEVADA
Baby by Chance—Elda Minger

29. NEW HAMPSHIRE
Sara's Father—Jennifer Mikels

30. NEW JERSEY
Tara's Child—Susan Kearney

31. NEW MEXICO
Black Mesa—Aimée Thurlo

32. NEW YORK
Winter Beach—Terese Ramin

33. NORTH CAROLINA
Pride and Promises—BJ James

34. NORTH DAKOTA
To Each His Own—Kathleen Eagle

35. OHIO
Courting Valerie—Linda Markowiak

36. OKLAHOMA
Nanny Angel—Karen Toller Whittenburg

37. OREGON
Firebrand—Paula Detmer Riggs

38. PENNSYLVANIA
McLain's Law—Kylie Brant

39. RHODE ISLAND
Does Anybody Know Who Allison Is?—Tracy Sinclair

40. SOUTH CAROLINA
Just Deserts—Dixie Browning

41. SOUTH DAKOTA
Brave Heart—Lindsay McKenna

42. TENNESSEE
Out of Danger—Beverly Barton

43. TEXAS
Major Attraction—Roz Denny Fox

44. UTAH
Feathers in the Wind—Pamela Browning

45. VERMONT
Twilight Magic—Saranne Dawson

46. VIRGINIA
No More Secrets—Linda Randall Wisdom

47. WASHINGTON
The Return of Caine O'Halloran—JoAnn Ross

48. WEST VIRGINIA
Cara's Beloved—Laurie Paige

49. WISCONSIN
Hoops—Patricia McLinn

50. WYOMING
Black Creek Ranch—Jackie Merritt

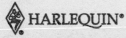 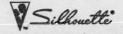

HARLEQUIN®   Silhouette®

Please address questions and book requests to: Harlequin Reader Service U.S.: 3010 Walden Ave.,
P.O. Box 1325, Buffalo, NY 14269 CAN.: P.O. Box 609, Fort Erie, Ont. L2A 5X3   PAHGEN

FOUR UNIQUE SERIES
FOR EVERY WOMAN YOU ARE...

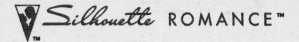

Silhouette ROMANCE™

These entertaining, tender and involving love stories
celebrate the spirit of pure romance.

Desire features strong heroes and spirited heroines
who come together in a highly passionate,
emotionally powerful and always provocative read.

Silhouette®SPECIAL EDITION®

For every woman who dreams of life, love and family,
these are the romances in which she makes
her dreams come true.

Dive into the pages of Intimate Moments and experience
adventure and excitement in these complex
and dramatic romances.

Silhouette ROMANCE™

What's a single dad to do when he needs a wife by next Thursday?

Who's a confirmed bachelor to call when he finds a baby on his doorstep?

How does a plain Jane in love with her gorgeous boss get him to notice her?

From classic love stories to romantic comedies to emotional heart tuggers, **Silhouette Romance** offers six irresistible novels every month by some of your favorite authors!

Such as...beloved bestsellers **Diana Palmer, Stella Bagwell, Sandra Steffen, Susan Meier** and **Marie Ferrarella,** to name just a few—and some sure to become favorites!

Silhouette Romance—always emotional, always enjoyable, always about love!